THAT'S THE WAY LOVE GOES

By Mark Marcus

Library of Congress Control Number: 2011938026

CANDLE SHORE PUBLISHING
4141 BALL ROAD SUITE 412
CYPRESS CALIFORNIA 90630
(702) 714-1545
candleshorepublishing.com

TABLE OF CONTENTS

PREFACE

"That's The Way Love Goes", as the title suggests, is a collection of short stories that explore and exalt the emotion of love in its most humbling arenas.

Each story is set in a world of unnamed characters who must deal with the inevitable trials and tribulations, rights and responsibilities, privileges and pitfalls of the universe's most compelling emotion.

Two people who want to become lost find each other in "The Meeting", a daughter forced to defend the greatest act of love in a courtroom in "The Witness", a prison guard who must rise above his station for humanity's sake in "The Letter", a young woman who must accept the events of her past so she can embrace the future in "Comin' Home", two ex-lovers who continue to fall into and out of each other's lives in "A Trip to Vaulden", a young boy leaving home cloaked only in the faith of his deceased grandmother in "Cameo", and an old bitter woman who witnesses her own birth in "The Cycle" are just a few examples of tales that will offer the reader a dazzling display of the human condition and the human heart as it struggles to balance the world in which we live and the world which lives within us.

This book sets itself apart from others in that it is based on the premise that it will be used as an emotional handbook of parables.

This book will appeal to all adults who need to know that they are not alone--not by any means, on this exciting and dangerous journey we call life.

FROM THE AUTHOR

You honor me by taking the time to read my words; thank you.

The following is a short message from my heart to yours:

Remember, love yourself as you love others and love others as you have never loved before.

Most Sincerely,

Mark

DEDICATION

This book is dedicated to those who never abandoned neither me nor their convictions for convenience sake and to those rare few people throughout my life who guided me by the light of their souls and the sincerity of their character.

A LITTLE HIGHER

I am thinking of you, today, and I smile. I smile as I
remember you, my untouched, unwrapped, and forever
unreachable one.

What do I remember? The way you look, the way you
sound, the ease with which you took my love to a higher
ground.

I remember the waxing of your flame, the waning of your
roar, and how the intensity of your gaze led my soul to a
higher floor.

You made me yours at the beginning, even from the
start, not with words or gestures but with the power of
your convictions that inflated and enraptured my all but
forgotten heart.

Being yours was uncertain, being yours was Hell, until
that moment when I realized that torment isn't so bad
when suffered at a higher level.

Do you think of me? For this I pray and for this I hope as
even the memory of you makes me feel as though I am
afloat, in a glorious chariot of fire.

I thank you, my darling, I thank you, my love, for sharing
the sweet and secret songs of your dreams and
emotions gifted by an angelic choir.

You are mine and mine alone, in the quiet still misty
midnight hour, for you and you alone dared enough,
cared enough to take me a little higher.

CAMEO

The sun is beginning to set now. As it slowly slides off its celestial perch, it casts a soft golden hue over a single set of railroad tracks that run through a tiny farming community. There are tall weeds on both sides of the tracks and he has to look down as he walks so as not to accidentally step on a snake.

He's walking now just passing time until he hears that powerful soft sweet rumble approaching from the distance. He's been walking along side the steel highway for a little over two hours now, walking, stepping, pushing his way through and waiting for the moment when he will jump on board that big black steam-driven chariot that will take him away from this place.

He had always been intrigued with the larger-than-life legend of the hobo. When he was younger, during summer thunderstorms, his grandmother would tell him stories about the almost mythical nomads as he sat at her feet wide-eyed and mesmerized.

As he steps over an old rotten log hidden deep within the recesses of the weeds, he realizes how much he misses her stories. Now, here he is just four days after his twelfth birthday, mere moments from hopping a freight train bound for the great unknown. He supposes that he isn't really going to become a real hobo just a stowaway for a few days until he reaches his destination, Crystal City, USA. Who knows, he may even make it all the way to Candleshore Beach, California, someday.

Two more hours pass.

The sun has long since set, now, and the sky is a dark grayish black as a young boy continues to push his way through thick foliage beside a set of seemingly abandoned railroad tracks.

Swush, swush, swush. The weeds, shoulder high now, brush against his face and he begins to itch. "The train," he says to himself as he moves through the darkness, "I've got to keep my mind on the train."

As he moves through the night, his thoughts return to his grandmother. He knows, even now as he strains his ears listening for any sign of the train, it is because of her and her alone that he has enough courage to leave home, to leave virtually all that he knows and everyone he loves so that he can make a good life for himself.

His grandmother had always favored him above his siblings. He has five brothers and sisters of whom he is the fourth youngest. He has good parents who treat his brothers and sisters and him equally in all things.

His grandmother, on the other hand, had always considered him special and unique. He had never taken her seriously when she would say things like, "Don't be sad, Sweetie, it's gonna be OK. Try to remember that you are different than the rest. You are a very unique and wonderful boy and many unique and wonderful things are waiting for you in your future."

It wasn't that his parents mistreated him or anything like that, nevertheless, they had never understood why he would rather read books and write stories than following in the footsteps of his older brothers by learning how to run the family farm with his father.

His grandmother, ah yes, she understood him like no other.

Cameo of a small child's body forcing its way through thick brush beside a set of cold and lonely railroad tracks. Both the boy and the tracks are cloaked in the blackness of the humid midwestern night. On the child's face tears begin to roll as he ponders the past. He remembers how his grandmother had smiled with warm approval each time he ran up to her carrying a new book he'd just received in the mail. While she herself could not read, she thoroughly enjoyed having others bring the written word to her by reading aloud. So, every evening for the past two years, after supper was finished and his daily chores completed, he would sit on her bed, American Indian style, and read to her as she lay beside him, listening intently.

Five hours now, five hours and still no sign of the train, no sign at all. He is starting to get worried now. He begins to question his decision to leave home in this way. What if the train doesn't come by, tonight, he wonders to himself as he peers, desperately, down the length of the tracks? What if it begins to rain out here or worse, hail? It often does at this time of year. It suddenly occurs to him how quickly the weather can change from good to bad. If the weather turns ugly he will find himself either being drenched in relentless sheets of falling water or being pummeled by fist-sized balls of falling ice. At this thought, he stops walking, touched by fear itself. He continues to stare down the length of the sleeping metal roadway and continues to see nothing, nothing whatsoever.

In the virtual silence of the night, he stands, motionless in the moment, too scared to go forward and too afraid to go back.

With uncertainty coursing along the emotional railroad tracks of his soul, he begins walking again, slower now so as to conserve energy. He begins searching now, searching for some kind, any kind of emotional anchor to grab onto so as not to sink even further into the ever strengthening quicksand of his doubt. He reaches into the front left pocket of his worn and tattered trousers and takes out his most valuable possession, his late grandfather's one and only pocket watch. His grandmother had secretly given it to him for his eleventh birthday.

Cameo of a young boy walking in the darkness of a warm midwestern night while holding a rather ancient looking timepiece that is almost too large for his preadolescent hand. He remembers his grandmother's words as she placed the last remaining possession of her late husband into her grandson's hand.

"Your granddaddy received this watch from his father, your great granddaddy, on his eleventh birthday, just like you. Your great granddaddy gave it to him the day before he left for the war. He told your grandfather that he purchased this watch on the eleventh day of the eleventh month of the eleventh year of the century. Your grandfather told me that he never saw his father again after that day, his eleventh birthday."

Cameo of a young boy placing a round object into his front left pant pocket as he walks in the night, an air of confidence slowly returning to his step.

One night, after reading a couple of pages from the Bible to her, she had said to him, "You know that I love you, don't you?" This question had made him feel uncomfortable. After all, he was eleven years old and, well, eleven-year-old guys just don't think about stuff like that.

After thinking about her question for a few seconds he'd replied, "Yes, I know you do, Gran." At that, she smiled, touched his little hand and said, "I believe in you and I know that you can go places with that mind of yours. It won't be easy for you. I'm afraid we haven't given you all the things a rich family could have given you. No matter, you have what it takes and you will make it out there."

At the time, he hadn't been sure of just what she was trying to tell him but now, oh yes, now he understood. He had asked, "Gran, I want to be a writer. Is that ridiculous?"

"No it's not, Baby," she had replied. "It's not at all. I know you'd be the best writer in the entire world. Remember, you can do anything you want if you want it badly enough. There will be many people in your life who will not believe in you. They will tell you to be happy with what you already have. But don't you believe them. You keep going, keep crawling, keep walking, keep running, pushing, keep learning and then challenging, keep stepping, keep climbing, and keep reaching until you touch the very stars, themselves."

To that he had replied, "Gran, no one can touch the stars." Her response to his statement had since become the source for many of his daydreams and night dreams. Positioning herself so that her right cheek was pressed against his right cheek so that their right eyes were mere inches from each other, she'd whispered in an unusually commanding voice that somehow still managed to be laced with love, "Find a way Boy. Do you hear me? You find a way to touch those stars and find a way to put one of them into your back pocket." With that, she'd sat back in her old rocking chair and the moment passed into history forever gone and forever burned into his soul.

But that moment, that perfect moment had come and gone a little over two months ago and his grandmother is dead now.

Five and a half hours now. He's been walking for five and a half hours and still no sign of the train. No train. It's so, so black and quiet out here. He looks up into the midnight sky and sees that the moon and her cousins have decided to stay in, tonight. The reality of what he is doing or, rather, trying to do plunges into his heart.

The wind picks up a bit and the temperature seems to be falling. He's cold and very hungry, now. Tears of sadness fill his tired eyes as he makes his way through the night.

"Take this to the table, boy," his mother commands, handing him a big bowl of green beans. It's suppertime and everyone, except his grandmother, is seated at the big wooden kitchen table. He takes the steaming bowl of beans from her and carries it over to the table. As he approaches, his youngest sister asks him, "Isn't that true?" Using both of her small plump hands, she brings a glass, which at one time during its existence had been a jelly jar, of milk up to her mouth and drinks.

"Isn't what true?" he replies.

"That you only read those stupid books to Gran and now that she's dead you're gonna throw them all away? That's what Daddy says," she answers, lowering her transparent goblet and carefully setting it back down on the table, just as she's been taught to do.

At hearing this, panic had gripped him as the meaning of her ever so innocently uttered words slam shut the door of hope his grandmother had worked so hard to open.

From across the kitchen his mother had confirmed, "Of course he's gonna throw them away. There are more important things around here that need doing than reading silly books." Approaching the table, herself, she finished, "We only bought them books for him so's he could entertain Gran. Now she's gone and those days are over for him. Now he's going to grow up the way the Lord intended him to, by working the land with his hands." His father had nodded in agreement.

It had been then and there that he finally realized, even in the warmth and safety of his family, he was a stranger in a strange land and that if he ever hoped to touch those stars for himself and for his grandmother, he would have to run away from home.

Now he's on the road, alone and on his own.

He pulls the bottom of his shirt up and wipes his eyes as he walks beside the railroad tracks. The weeds have given way to low brush now. This allows him to doze as he moves threw the darkness.

Finally, reluctantly, after walking seven and a half hours he stops walking and crumples to the ground. Sleep; all he wants now is to sleep.

His head begins to fall forward, eyes closing when he hears something in the distance. The sound is so faint at first that his slumbering mind almost dismisses it as nothing more than the wind. Then he remembers and forces his eyes open and raises his head to listen.

"It's here! It's here!" he exclaims into the night. The sound of the steam engine cuts through the silence of the night, awakening it and what had mere moments before been a proverbial gloomy valley of defeat is now a glorious mountain of victory.

He jumps to his feet and as he does, his heart somersaults into his throat. "It's really here," he says to himself.

He's on his way, at last, at last he's on his way. As the boy listens to the roaring engine, a new kind of fear touches him. Unlike his original fear, however, this one is a good fear. It's an expectant fear.

There! He can see the bright yellow glow of the headlight coming out of the darkness. He thinks it's the most beautiful thing he's ever seen. As the corona of the glorious blinding light grows larger and larger, the sound of the engine becomes louder and louder. He looks down at his legs and marvels at the sight of his trousers being bathed in that wonderful light.

Closer, closer, and closer still. Please come closer, just a little closer. The young man-child experiences an almost uncontrollable urge to start jumping up and down and shouting at the top of his lungs.

Less than half a mile away, now.

WUUUUUUUUUHHH--- wuuuu--- wuuuuh!

The whistle blows and the air around him is electrified with power and wonder and awe. The train is here. He grabs his dirty, brown satchel and steps up to the tracks.

WUUUUUUWUUWUUUUUWUUU-- WUUUUU-UU!

He jumps.

8

Cameo of a young boy leaping on to a roaring black mass of moving, vibrating steel wrapped in hot powerful swirling steam. The boy's eyes are wide with excitement. He is dressed in simple farm clothes but there is nothing simple about the expression on his face. His expression is one of deep and unyielding determination.

As his one hundred and twenty pound body lands on board the speeding ebony colossus, he remembers his grandmother and knows that this is all happening because of her. He will never doubt her words or himself again.

As he sits on the cold metal floor of the second to last car of the train, he closes his eyes and whispers out loud, "I'm going to touch those stars for you, Gran. I promise."

He doesn't know what tomorrow will bring but it doesn't matter. All things are possible, now. Eyes closed, he hears his grandmother's words:

Son, all any of us really need is love. Love is its own beginning and its own end.

Love is its own prize and its own consolation.

Love is unreasonable and melodramatic. In fact, love demands the dramatic.

None of us can possess love, in fact, we are quite powerless against it. Love, however, can quite easily possess us and by so doing give us the power to move mountains if we so choose.

Love is never the answer but always the question.

We cannot destroy love. It, however, can effortlessly destroy us.

Sitting on the cold metal floor, beginning to nod off to sleep, he recalls how she always ended her talks with him, "Love makes all things possible, because, when it's all said and done, Baby, That's The Way Love Goes."

THE MEETING

They roll passionately on the bedroom floor. They are both lost in the rapture of the moment, in the act at hand. Neither can believe this is happening; but it is, without a doubt, happening. It is, in a word, wonderful, and more glorious than any dream.

Las Vegas can be an exciting place especially to those who have never danced cheek-to-cheek with its dark lustful soul. It is many things to many people for many reasons; to some it is a technicolor playground filled with endless neon-bathed wonder and to others a relentless raging inferno of forbidden temptation and despair. To him, it is just a weekend away from the normal tortures of life in Barstow, California. One month ago he and an old buddy had decided to meet there and like everything else in his life, all had gone according to plan. It had been a long time since he and his old high school pal had seen each other, seven years to be exact. Yes, everything had gone according to plan, almost.

As she leaves the casino after another long hard shift of dealing cards, she thinks to herself, "Tonight is the last night I'm working here." She hates working in casinos most of which are located in the gross bellies of nightmarishly egocentric architectural monstrosities whose outrageous room rates she could never hope to afford. She has come to loathe the seemingly endless wave of tourists who crash down over the Strip every single night; she hates their inflated egos, their low-budget tips, their disgusting backroom habits and humor, and most of all their puerile ability to blame her when they lose all their money at the table. She is a card dealer and although she thought she had prepared herself for the realities of living in the largest money-driven entertainment Mecca in the world, she had not, it seemed, prepared herself well enough.

It had been one year ago almost to the day that she had stepped off the Greyhound bus in Las Vegas, Nevada. It had been a long journey from Madisonville, Kentucky but she had made it. As she steps onto the escalator leading down to the south side exit she remembers her almost uncontrollable exhilaration at seeing, for the first time, what seemed like an endless carnival of lights that is, for better or worse, Las Vegas. For her, a wide-eyed Midwestern girl, it had been a once in a lifetime moment. That had been one year ago and now, as BB King soulfully wails in his legendary blues song, "The thrill is gone."

Now she is a dealer in a casino and now, once again, she hates her life. It's two am, Friday morning when she walks through the revolving door exit of the hotel. As the warm desert wind kisses her sad and tired face she thinks, "It's going to be a boring weekend."

No one in Las Vegas noticed when on a warm Saturday evening at approximately seven pm a rather plain-featured young woman walking briskly down Flamingo Boulevard, not paying attention to anything in particular, bumped into two casually dressed well-groomed young men, apparently in deep discussion, walking in the opposite direction. No one in Las Vegas noticed when one of the young men instinctively reached out and touched her on the shoulder to keep her from stumbling. No one could tell that both of their hearts skipped a beat when their bodies made contact for the first time; certainly not the young man's companion.

They, however, noticed; the man and woman who met each other on that beautiful wonderful warm sweet Saturday Vegas evening. They would talk about it for many, many years to come for you see, "That's The Way Love Goes."

A DAYDREAM

My Love:

Do you know where I am now?

I am in a daydream of you and me being together; being together as the tom-toms play.

We are tied together beyond any untying for I am inside you and you, inside me; inside me as the tom-toms play.

We are swimming through the seas of life, occasionally glimpsing distant islands of uncertainty that keep us not from our destiny of living, laughing, lusting, loving; yes loving, as the tom-toms play.

Here, time is only a whisper, sorrow but a speck of dust in the wake of the whisper and pain merely an ancient mirage.

Blackness, whiteness, red green yellow and blueness caress us, embrace us, slip slide and go through us as we glide into each other's light.

We say nothing for words are not enough, feelings are not enough, thoughts are not enough; not even the glory of heaven is enough to capture the power of our love; a power that can only be expressed as the tom-toms play.

Oh My Sweet Baby, wish for me and I will wish for you; for upon that wish our journey will, one day, start.

And as I wake from my daydream I, at long last, discover that the deep, steady, and forever unending sound of the tom-toms is the music you bring to my ever waiting heart.

My Love:
 Do you know where I am now?

CHANCES

The wind sings softly as they walk back to her car. It's dark and cool tonight at the beach. As they walk, the back of her left hand brushes against the back of his right. The cool Candleshore Beach air is filled with the sweet smell of cotton candy and freshly fried doughnuts. In spite of the seaside aromas, the scent of her perfume manages to tickle the end of his nose.

As they make their way through the tiny maze of seemingly sleeping cars, he thinks about his grandmother--how she would have loved the beach. He is almost certain that she had never been to the coast. What a shame that she had passed away before he could bring her here, what a shame.

She is saying something to him as they walk but her voice is little more than that of a faint instrument in the symphony of his thoughts. "I've got to pay attention to what she is saying so I won't be caught off guard in case she asks me something," he thinks to himself.

Click, click, click. He looks up at the full misty milk moon and, in his mind, tries to imagine what the sound of her heels, as they kiss the pavement, would look like if he could see as well as hear them.

He likes this girl--he really does, he just can't figure out where on this, their first date, things had gone wrong.

"And so I think I'll be out of town for a while," she finishes. He nods his head but has absolutely no idea what she is talking about.

It must have been over dessert, he thinks to himself-- yeah, that was when he'd known that this evening was going to be a bust.

"But I really had a good time I just don't think, well, what do you think?"

He catapults himself back to the moment at hand. They are standing next to her white Mazda Protege, facing each other.

Short gusts of wind spray sand at them.

Taking her lead he says in a comedic fashion, "Well, we're both nice people aren't we?" He widens his eyes as if to say, "See, I'm still game if you are."

A gentle smile crosses her face. She has such a lovely smile and it makes him want to be close to her.

As they stand there, each waiting for the other to speak, he realizes that he likes the fact that, even in heels, she is slightly shorter than he.

Her dark brown eyes, large in the moonlight, stare at him and for a moment, a very brief and breathless moment, he wants to dive into them.

This is the moment, the dreaded and sought after moment that all men and women who skulk through the darkest regions of the dating jungle must face, sooner or later. Yes, this is it, the moment when two people will either go boldly into steamy romance or crawl reluctantly into platonic friendship.

Another gust of wind, sand in their eyes, more sand, and then the wind and the moment pass, together.

They raise their hands to their eyes and, squinting, begin to remove the tiny particles, eyes watering now.

Why is he not letting this go? he wonders to himself as he lowers his hands. He knows that they are not right for each other but instead of saying, "Well, I think we need to keep searching," here he is mere seconds away from kissing this woman.

"I had a nice time with you," he says, breaking the silence between them.

Almost bird-like, she leans up and forward and gives him a quick peck on the cheek and then, almost as suddenly, turns her body away from him. Bringing her purse up between them, she begins searching for her keys.

He steps back to give her room. The night, itself, constructs a thin but impenetrable invisible wall between them.

A thin stream of gas escapes him, a sign that in about five minutes he will need to find a restroom.

"Well," she says extracting the keys from the deep recesses of her purse, "I'll give you a call when I get back into town, maybe, OK?"

Digging deep into his own pocket for his own set of keys, he says, "That sounds great."

An awkward silence.

"Would you like me to get your door for you?" he asks reaching for her keys.

"No, I've got it, take care and good luck."

He watches the little shiny white Protege back out of the slumbering beachside parking lot and turn north onto Catalina Avenue. At the traffic light, it stops for a brief moment and then turns east onto Torrance Boulevard and disappears.

Cold keys in hand, he turns back towards the water and listens to the ocean. His ocean, as he has come to think of it, sounds so sad and so very lonely, tonight, just like he himself feels.

"What the hell!" he exclaims to himself and begins walking towards the boardwalk which parallels the silky blue waters of Candleshore Beach, California.

Yep, it had been over dessert--that was when everything had fallen apart on this, their first and apparently only date.

He found it hard to believe that they had met each other online only two short weeks earlier. Wow! They'd come a long way since then. He had answered her ad and she, in turn, had sent him a warm reply. Everyday since then they had been in contact with each other either by email or telephone.

There it is, that old familiar sinking feeling right in the middle of his chest, the feeling of loss.

His bladder tries to get his attention by churning a little in his groin but he wills it into submission.

He is less than ten feet from the water's edge, now, walking in the moonlight, thinking about the evening's earlier events.

They had decided to meet at the Candleshore Beach pier and have dinner at a popular local bistro called Ernie's At The Pier.

The first part of the evening had gone well. They had discussed topics that thirty-year-olds usually discuss on first dates, past relationships, children, career goals, food, music, foreplay, and so on.

It seemed to him that the longer they spent in each other's presence the closer they became, spiritually at least.

After they are seated in a nice tucked-away corner of the restaurant, they begin reading their menus. After a minute or so he asks her what she intends to order. She responds, "Oh, this is your town and your restaurant, I'll have whatever you're having. See, I trust you already." They both laugh.

He sits upon a low gray brick wall and stares out at the dark Pacific Ocean. The distant moon looks down upon him and sheds one tear on his behalf.

Their table is cleared and they lean forward towards each other, getting closer. The restaurant is wonderfully warm and cozy.

He reaches out and brushes one strand of shiny black hair away from her cheek.

He should have kissed her then, he thinks to himself, sitting on the wall, he should have taken her round soft-featured face into his hands and kissed her right then and there. He hadn't, though, and the moment, the perfect moment had come and gone in an instant.

"Will you be having dessert tonight, Sir?" the waiter asks. They lean back in their seats, the warmth of her nearness deserting him. He was preparing to say, no to the idiot waiter when she, his date, said quite definitely, "Yes, we will. His mouth, forming the word "no," snaps shut.

"Do you serve tiramisu?" she asks, politely.

"Yes," the waiter answers. "And for you, Sir?" he asks.

"Just bring two forks," he answers rather abruptly.

An old man and his equally old black Labrador stroll very slowly on the boardwalk. It is clear, to anyone who notices, that they have absolutely nowhere to go, that they are just marking time. They pass in front of a man sitting on a low gray brick wall, bathed in the moonlight.

The man on the wall swings his legs back and forth, back and forth, back and forth as he stares into the distance. His eyes do not focus on the old man and his four-legged companion. In fact, he hardly notices them as they cross his field of vision. The movie of the evening's earlier events is still playing in his mind and all he can see is her, his date, as she takes a fork full of the sweet dessert and places it ever so lightly on the tip of his tongue.

"Why, thank you," he says after swallowing. "I haven't been fed since I was a young boy.

"Well," she begins, "stick with me and you're going to have a lot of experiences that you haven't had since you were a young boy, well, since you were a teenager at least." A sly gleam appears in her eyes. She brings the fork up to her lips, pauses, and then makes the Italian delight disappear.

The man on the wall smiles.

Wiping his mouth he asks, "So, where do we go from here?"

Lightly touching her mouth with her own napkin, she answers softly, "I just don't know, back to my place and to bed?" They both laugh, a little uncomfortably.

"I don't know what is going to happen but I need to tell you something," she adds.

"OK, what?"

A second old man, with a dark red yoyo in hand, walks in front of a man, sitting on a wall with a harsh look on his face. The old man stops for a moment and considers asking the man on the wall if he is OK. As he opens his mouth to speak, the man on the wall raises his left hand, makes a tight fist, and slams it down onto his leg. As the old man watches the human anvil fall, he expects to hear a sound like that of raw meat being slapped but there is no sound as it makes contact with its target; there is only the sound of the wind. The old man decides to say nothing and continue with his walk.

"Well the last two weeks have been great, for me at least, and I just want to be completely honest with you so we can move forward," she says.

Feeling like a father listening to his little girl preparing to confess some overwhelming secret, he says, "OK, tell me, I'll understand. Give me your hand."

She rests her elbows on the now cleared dining table and extends her hands to him.

"I've decided that I want a normal heterosexual relationship with a man but I want you to know that, well, this is a relatively recent decision.

That was when it had happened--right then and there. Why had she told him about it, then? Why had she not told him about this during one of their many telephone conversations?

The mental playback grinds to a halt in his mind.

The man on the wall stands, mouths the words "sweet Jesus" to himself, shakes his head slowly, and then heads for home.

1

Lee Smith powers up his home PC for the first time in two weeks. Coincidentally, the exact same amount of time has passed since his last date at the Candleshore Beach pier.

After returning home and emptying his aching bladder, that night, he'd actually considered getting right back online and trying, yet again, to make another love connection with someone else. In fact, he had gone so far as turning his computer on but just as its BIOS informed him that all of its sixty-four megabytes of RAM had successfully checked in for duty, his stomach had begun to bloat and a feeling of overwhelming depression and disgust for the PC, the Internet and everything else for that matter, engulfed him and so he had abruptly turned the machine off and gone to bed.

Now, two weeks later, here he was again, sitting in the same old brown wooden chair, that he had lifted from a former place of employment, in his home office.

With the click of the mouse he logs onto the One For One Internet dating site for singles. Lee is online, reaching out, again.

2

AD

CHANCES

Yes, I guess it's just like my ad says, I take chances as you can tell by the simple fact that this ad is even here.

A friend of mine told me that when placing an ad I should list all of my best qualities, so, here it goes: I am simply wonderful! (Big Smile.)

What am I looking for? I am looking for a nice guy who knows himself and knows his place in the universe. I seek a guy who will not automatically place me at the center of his world but will do so upon request. This may sound mean but if you have any unresolved issues, please don't expect me to resolve them for you.

So, if you are the man of my dreams, send me a reply.

kk
PS
No married men need apply.

3

Lee finishes reading the ad entitled Chances; so many ads trying to be a little bit funny and a little bit sexy and a little bit serious all at the same time.

He had wanted to place an ad of his own for a long time but he could never sum up enough courage. He just couldn't stand the thought of putting an SOS out there only to have no one respond.

He reads two more ads and then decides to go to bed.

4

At 1:30 am. Lee sits in front of his computer and logs on to One For One. "Here I am again," he thinks to himself, "tossing bottles into the Cyber Sea."

As he reads ad, after ad, after ad, he begins thinking about one ad in particular, the one he had come across a few days ago. He decides to re-read it again.

Two hours later, after reading what seems like an endless stream of cyber rubbish, he finally finds the ad he seeks. Yes, here it is, entitled, CHANCES.

He reads it several times and while reading, measures himself against the yardstick described by kk.

One thing he notices about kk's ad is that it, unlike many others, does not say that he need be financially secure-- not that he is exactly poor but he does have to watch every dollar, these days. Kk's ad does not inform him of her location on the globe, either, however. The idea of starting a correspondence with someone living halfway across the country or worse, halfway around the world is not exactly enticing to Lee. After a bit more deliberation, he decides to respond to Kk's SOS.

5

At 3:07 am. Saturday morning, a rather average looking man, sitting in front of his home PC whispers to himself, "OK, I'm going to do it." The man's hands, poised over the keyboard, look like a cameo of two dolphins frozen in a downward arc. Finally, the cameo is shattered as the dolphins fall to the calm mechanical sea of keys and the man begins to type.

6

DAY ONE

From: mailbox 8888

To: mailbox 1619

Subject: Chances

Hi kk,

Well, I'm taking a chance just like you. It's not easy but I'm here and I liked your ad. I've always wanted to meet a simply wonderful woman.

Are you still searching for someone special?

Ls

DAY TWO

From: mailbox 1619

To: mailbox 8888

Subject: Re: Chances

Hey there ls.

Yes, I'm still looking. So who are you and where are you located?
kk

DAY THREE

From: mailbox 8888

To: mailbox 1619

Subject: Who Am I?

Hi kk,

Well, I live in Candleshore Beach, which is just down the road from LAX. Where do you live/work/exist?

Who am I? Well, I'm a guy who manages a small mom and pop computer repair shop. I have two cats, Amy and Rosalie. I love them both very much. I love to read, hate to cook, love to fish, hate to swim, love to dance, hate to dance alone.

Now, it's your turn.

ls

DAY FOUR

From: mailbox 1619

To: mailbox 8888

Subject: Re: Who Am I?

I see. Well, I've heard of Redondo Beach, Hermosa Beach, and Manhattan Beach but I've never heard of Candleshore Beach. I'll take your word as to its location on the planet. (Smile.)

You are emailing a woman in San Diego, California. I am a Generation "Y" baby. I am a registered nurse. No, I don't work in a hospital. I am a private care nurse.

Let's see, I love to sing, hate to clean, love to jog, hate to swim, love to drive, hate to skate, love to eat, hate to gain weight, love to travel, hate to travel alone.

kk
PS
I like the way you did that love/hate thing. It's very cute. I'll use it from now on.

Thank you, Mr. Candleshore.

PPS

What is your name, first name at least? My first name is Katelyn but everyone calls me Katy.

DAY FIVE

From: mailbox 8888

To: mailbox 1619

Subject: Re: Re: Who Am I?

Thank you for the compliment. My first name is Lee. It's pretty simple, I know, but it's mine.

I see you like to sing. I do, too. I'm not very good but I try every now and then. What kind of music do you like to sing?

I like San Diego. I used to live there about five or so years ago. It was home to me for a while. I miss it. Life is definitely more complicated up here in Los Angeles County.

I am originally from Madisonville, Tennessee.

How about you? Where are you from, originally?

Work was not fun today. The owners, Ma and Pa as I call them, must have had a fight last night because when they came in this morning there was tension between them.

You know, even when they're mad at each other they always maintain their daily routine. For example, she still gets him his morning coffee and he still walks down the street to buy her a candy bar at lunchtime.

I don't know about you but I like the fact that a mere spat doesn't cause their normal routine to break down. I hope that someday I'll meet someone with whom I will feel as secure.

LS

DAY SIX

From: mailbox 1619

To: mailbox 8888

Subject: Interesting

Pleasure to make your acquaintance, Mr. Candleshore Lee.

I am originally from San Francisco.

Tennessee, eh? Wow! You are a long way from home. What brought you out here?

Why am I in San Diego? I was married once and his job transferred him here. So, when we divorced I decided to stay. See, it's all very simple.

I like to sing popular songs, no operas or operettas for me. (Smile.)

Have you ever been married? I hope the fact that I have been does not scare you off. If it does, however, I will certainly understand. He no longer lives here. His job eventually transferred him to Little Rock. I know you're wondering so let me tell you the answer is no, I have no children with him or anyone else for that matter, at least, none that I know of, anyway. (Smile.)

Baring one's soul is so draining. (Wink.)

I think it's so sweet that Ma and Pa, as you call them, continue their daily routines. That's what it's all about, when you're with someone you know loves you and still wants to lie down beside you at night no matter what happened during the day.

Mr. Lee, I've never experienced such a relationship.

Write Soon,

Lee sits at his computer thinking about Katelyn's last email to him. He considers the fact that she was once married. He himself has never been married. Hadn't he heard that a marriage has an even greater chance of failing when one of the spouses has a previously failed marriage?

Marriage? Here he is, just barely into a new electronic correspondence relationship and he is, thinking about marriage. These thoughts go through his mind as he leans back in his chair staring at her message on the computer screen.

Well, it wasn't as if she and her ex-husband had any children together.

A smile crosses his face as he sits up in his chair and thinks to himself, "Well, it's all about chances, right?"

DAY SEVEN

From: mailbox 8888

To: mailbox 1619

Subject: Why I'm Here

Hi Katy,

First off, let me assure you that I have no problem with the fact that you've been married once before. At least I think it's once, right? (Smile.)

I, myself, have never been married. Hum, I wonder if that says something about me. No, I'm not a mama's boy. I promise.

Well, I came out here seeking fortune and fame just like everyone else. It didn't work out but I couldn't go home because I burned a few too many bridges, if you know what I mean. So, it was either sink or swim and I've always wanted to learn how to do the backstroke. Now I live here in Candleshore Beach.

So, are you a good nurse?

Write Soon,

LS

8

From: mailbox 1619

To: mailbox 8888

Subject: Bad Day and What?

What a crappy day! I won't bore you with the details but sometimes I get sick and tired of hearing my patients constantly complaining even when there is nothing medically wrong with them.

Am I a good nurse? Yes, I think I am even though I don't feel like one all the time. I genuinely like being around people and I like helping them when I can. Do I enjoy wiping peoples' butts? No, I most certainly do not. Nevertheless, I enjoy helping people, my patients, get better.

When I was a little girl I wanted to be a ballerina, of course, because I thought it would make people feel better. Watching people dance always made me feel better so I thought I could do the same for others.

Well, to make an even longer story longer still, a world-class ballerina I ain't but a world-class healthcare professional, I am, indeed.

So, tell me, Mr. Candleshore Lee, what are you looking for in a relationship?

Please tell me the truth and be specific. I am sick and tired of hearing the same old standard answers like happiness and world peace. I mean, who wouldn't want those things, right?

We've been writing for a little over a week now and I think we need to see where we stand on some issues. So, you first and then me, OK?

Kk
PS
I see that you did not tell me whether or not you yourself have any children out there, interesting. (Smile.)

DAY NINE

No reply.

DAY TEN

From: mailbox 8888

To: mailbox 1619

Subject: Here It Is?

First off, let me tell you here and now that I do not have any children. However, were I to find the right lady, I'd like to have one or two little versions of myself running up and down the seashore.

Please forgive me for not writing yesterday but I wanted to give you an honest, unrehearsed answer. So, as the subject line above reads, here it is:

I want a normal one-on-one relationship with a kind lady. I want the kind of relationship that can and, most likely will, lead to marriage. I know that probably sounds funny coming from a guy but, then again, you asked for the complete and total truth.

I would like to meet a woman who does not have hundreds of little skeletons in her proverbial closet such as illicit drug use, criminal incarceration, topless dancing, or any other number of sins against society.

I would like to meet a woman not hell-bent on having children just because her friends have them and she feels it would make her feel better about herself. If we are to have a child, I want him or her to be the result of our love and not because he or she will provide some kind of security in our relationship.

I would like to meet a woman who is intelligent but not so arrogant with her intelligence that she beats me over the head with it at every opportunity. I would like to meet a lady who says what she means and means what she says. I seek a woman who knows what she wants but will not hurt those she loves in order to get it.

I would love to meet someone who will tell me when I'm wrong but will do so only in private.

I would like to meet a lady who can lead as well as follow.

I would like to meet someone who will not expect me to atone for the wrongs done to her by previous partners. I make enough of my own mistakes in romantic relationships without having to apologize for the faux pas of others.

Is that honest enough for you? I think you get the idea.

Now, it's your turn.

LS

9

Lee leans back in his chair, emotionally drained. Boy! He really put it out there this time, he thinks to himself.

He turns off the computer monitor and closes his eyes.

He decides to go get something from the fridge, a bottle of soda or a glass of milk, anything to take his mind off of what he has just sent to Katy.

He wonders if she will reply today or tomorrow or ever, for that matter.

Two hours pass.

Lee fires up his PC and downloads his email. There it is, a reply from Katy.

He begins to read:

From: mailbox 1619

To: mailbox 8888

Subject: Re: Here It Is?

Hello Dear Mr. Lee,

Well, I'm not looking for a knight in shining armor but I would like a man who will stand with me and by me and for me should there be a need to do so. I want to be with a man who does not try to fix my life or make it into what he thinks it should be. I am not perfect but I do seek perfection; that's always been good enough for me and it should be good enough for him.

I tend to be habitually late for appointments so I want a man who understands that this is not likely to change anytime soon.

To be quite honest, I want to fall in love with a man who is good with his hands, better with his mind, and best with his heart.

I know that guys don't like talking about their feelings, be that as it may, I want to be with a man who doesn't mind discussing mine and, better yet, I want a man who isn't afraid to take out his own feelings and polishing them off once in while.

Not once in all the years that I lived with my parents did I ever hear my father apologize to my mother, no matter how wrong he discovered he had been. Now don't get me wrong, he would make amends to her by more promptly completing household projects she assigned him or by surprising her with some trinket she had seen and admired in some store window with the explanation, "I stopped by that store again and it was on sale," or by being unusually polite to her; but never and I mean never did he ever give her a direct apology. I think that is sad.

I want someone who can make a direct unsolicited apology when he knows he's been wrong. Can you do that, Mr. Candleshore?

I want to be with someone who will always be honest with me but not so honest that it becomes cruel. I like men who like children and little cats and dogs.

I know that guys like to be independent but when that independence causes someone to worry unnecessarily, then that so-called independence is nothing more than thoughtlessness and selfishness, plain and simple. So, for me, he has to be considerate and loving.

From time-to-time I need my own personal time alone. I would like to meet someone who will accommodate this facet of my personality.

I am not a "daddy's girl" and I don't want to be with a "mama's boy."

I've dated a couple of guys who tried to get me to change my career. They hated the fact that I am a nurse because they didn't like the idea of me seeing naked men. Honest, they just couldn't get used to the idea. I love being a nurse and I have no plans to stop being one, anytime soon.

Well, Mr. Candleshore Lee, are you still listening? Are you still interested in me? I guess we're reaching the crossroads here, eh?

Write Soon,

Katy
PS
I don't want a man with cold feet, either. (Smile.)

DAY ELEVEN

From: mailbox 1619

To: mailbox 8888

Subject: Are you Ready?

Lee, I think I'd like to talk to you on the phone and hear your voice. Here is my home phone number. The best time to catch me this week is either before seven in the morning or after nine at night. OK, my number is (619) 111-6275.

Katy

DAY TWELVE

No reply.

DAY THIRTEEN

10

As the bus turns west on to Torrance Boulevard, headed for the Candleshore Beach pier, Lee Smith is sitting in his usual starboard side seat staring through the lightly tented window.

"Well," he thinks to himself, "the time has finally come again." It's been two days since Katy emailed her telephone number to him. Why hadn't he called her, yet, he asks himself? In his heart he knows the answer. The reason he hasn't called is because he has discovered time and time again that, most often, the illusion of a woman is better than the woman, herself, and he doesn't want his beautifully glorious neon image of her shattered by reality.

"Next stop Hawthorne Boulevard. Hawthorne Boulevard, next stop," an automated voice says, cheerfully, over the loudspeaker. The bus jerks to a halt and three rather dumpy looking boys exit the bus immediately followed by two elderly ladies, who board. The bus driver, Lee can't remember her name, waits patiently as they show their bus passes and seat themselves in the seats reserved for senior or handicapped passengers. The bus begins to roll.

Lee's mind takes on two personas to, once again, allow his two closest friends, Mr. Pro and Mrs. Con, to enter into a discussion. The debate between them begins:

11

"Lee Boy, you've got to call her. You know that don't you?" Mr. Pro begins.

"But what if she turns out to be like that other girl, you know, the one who made that recent decision?" Mrs. Con asks.

Mr. Pro says, sternly. "Lee, what in the hell is life without love? What is life without taking chances? I'll tell you, it's death."

Mrs. Con asks Mr. Pro, "Why must you always be so melodramatic? I'm not saying this girl is weird or anything but think of all the energy it takes to pick up that phone and take that chance yet again. The boy needs to focus on his career and making money so he will have a nice nest-egg for when he's older."

Lee, eyes closed, slightly sways back and forth as the automated announcer informs him that Prospect Avenue is the next stop.

"Chances," Mr. Pro says with a huff, "are what it's all about. Without chances there is no hope, no future, and no end in sight. Taking chances is what separates those who have from those who have not. Love is worth any and all risks for without love we are reduced to mere mortals, forever searching, forever hurting, forever alone. I know there are those who truly enjoy being alone but I don't think our Lee, here, is one of them. He wants more than money and he wants more than fame. He wants to love and to be loved. Come to think of it, he probably wouldn't mind a little sex along the way, either, right, Big Guy?"

Lee smiles to himself, on the bus.

Mr. Pro continues, "When it's all said and done, our Lee, here, believes in chances and he believes in women. Now isn't that right, Lee Boy?"

Lee silently mouths the words, "I don't know anymore. I just don't know anymore."

"Of course you don't know, Honey," Mrs. Con says, sounding a lot like Lee's dead grandmother. "You've been disappointed so many times and you're tired of being hurt," she finishes, empathetically.

To Mr. Pro, Mrs. Con says sharply, "And stop being vulgar!"

"Tired my ... butt," Mr. Pro retorts, equally as sharply and sounding more and more like Lee's old high school wrestling coach, Lance Mann.

"Lee, Boy," Mr. Pro continues, "if you're going to be tired of anything be tired of these endless debates with yourself."

Eyes still closed, Lee nods his head as the bus continues its journey down Torrance Boulevard.

"Next stop, Candleshore Beach. Candleshore Beach, next stop."

As Lee opens his eyes and pulls the stop-cord, he faintly hears Mr. Pro say, "Lee, Boy, it's all about chances, taking chances, OK? Remember, it's all about reaching for the stars and taking chances, chance is all there is."

The bus stops and Lee stands up.

He nods to the short-haired and rather busty bus driver and steps off the coach. He heads for home, ready to make the call and take a chance.

12

Lee's hands are somewhat clammy as he dials the telephone number he copied from his computer screen. He presses the receiver close to his face so as to hear the ringing on the other end. After the third ring the phone is answered and a female voice says, "Hello?"

Taking a deep breath, Lee replies cautiously, "Hello, may I speak to Katelyn?" His throat feels kind of scratchy but he doesn't want to clear it just yet.

"This is she," the voice quickly replies.

Inwardly, Lee smiles for the voice on the other end is soft and somewhat sultry not unlike that of Lauren Bacall. Sensing that he may be taking too long to reply, he says, "Hi Katelyn, this is Lee, you know, the guy you've been emailing from Candleshore Beach?"

Her response is excited and noticing this makes Lee feel so very good and much more confident. She says, "Oh, hi Lee. I'm so glad you called. You know it's been several days since I heard from you. Are you OK?"

Lee is touched by her question. How thoughtful of her to ask, he thinks to himself. He is amazed at how much her question moves him. At hearing her question, the gatekeeper to Lee's heart, who has been so very diligent in performance of its duty, bows its head and quietly, graciously steps aside and Lee feels his heart begin to open to her.

Clearing his throat and purposely lowering the pitch of his voice so as to sound more "manly," he says, "Oh I'm fine, thank you."

"Well," she begins, "it looks like we've taken yet another step forward, eh?" To Lee, this conversation feels more like a grand leap rather than a meager step.

"So, tell me something?" she asks, enthusiastically.

A feeling of hope and excitement begin to stir within him and it feels as though his soul is being cleansed by a wave of fresh clean spring water.

Lee says, "Well, I guess we have, at that. Like they say, it's all about taking chances."

13

The room is dim, comfortably warm, and cozy. The air is filled with the dark sweet fragrance of her perfume. They lay on the bed, uncovered and naked; neither has spoken for several minutes. Each is contemplating what is about to take place. There is music and its low, slow, smooth staccato rhythmic drumbeat caresses the floor, the walls, the unusually low ceiling, the bed, their very souls causing their hearts to beat as one.

She gently touches his cheek with a fair, delicate finger and brings her lips to his and presses carefully, softly. The kiss, the length of which seems to last an eternity and the grace of which propels them both into the most erotic regions of romance, is all consuming and it quickly engulfs them, wraps them both in an envelope of white hot fire. Their tongues meet in the ever-waxing tempest of passion. Time stands still. Then, the tongues begin to dance the dance of intense lust to the rhythm of the tom-toms. She pulls him even closer to her and lies back on the dark blue satin sheets.

And the tom-toms play.

She gently guides his hand down to her private place
that only the tom-toms can see. A soft sigh escapes her.

And the toms-toms play. And the tom-toms play.

14

Lee awakens in his same old bed, alone and sweating.
The dream is over.

DAY NINETY

15

As Lee takes his seat on the Boeing 737, heading to Las
Vegas, his thoughts are racing with the anticipation of
what he is doing.

It has been two months since his first telephone call to
Katy. So far, so good.

After two months of daily telephone conversations,
emails, and several weekend dates in either San Diego
or Candleshore Beach, they had decided to take a short
trip together. Actually, it had been Katelyn's idea but
Lee had gladly agreed to it. As it turned out, Katy had
never been to Las Vegas and Lee hadn't been there in
over ten years, himself.

As the plane begins to taxi, nearing its lift-off point, Lee
feels at one with the aircraft as he, too, is nearing a lift-
off point in the flight that is his life.   As the 737 rises
from the earth and begins its climb into the deep dark
velvet blue night sky, a feeling of confident giddiness
washes over Lee and he is suddenly certain, without a
shadow of a doubt, that he and Katy are doing the right
thing, the good thing, the only thing.

The plane banks to the left and Lee feels so very good.

Lee closes his eyes and for the first time in a long time Mr. Pro and Mrs. Con pay him a visit and begin to speak in his mind.

"I am so proud of you, Lee Boy. You've come a long way, baby," Mr. Pro says encouragingly.

"Now, now," Mrs. Con cautions, "don't push him. He's still got some doubts and that's good."

"There's no time for doubts. By the way, Lee, good idea getting adjacent rooms, you know, one common door and all. Brilliant! Hubba, hubba!" he exclaims.

Mrs. Con says, sullenly, "That's disgusting."

Eyes closed, Lee smiles at their dialogue.

"Looking forward to your trip, Sir?"

Lee's eyes snap open and he sits up in his seat. Looking down at him is a very lovely flight attendant. Her nametag reads Barbie.

Lee says, "Pardon?"

"I didn't mean to disturb you. You had a big smile on your face."

Lee grins and says, "Oh, yes, I am looking forward to this trip. I'm off on an adventure."

Lee can smell the light aroma of Barbie's perfume, jasmine.

Barbie says, excitedly, "Wow! A real adventure? I am so jealous. Why are you going on this adventure, Sir?"

Lee thinks for a moment and then replies, thoughtfully, "Because it's time I take a chance--no, because I think I'm in love."

"I'm so happy for you. She must be quite a lady," Barbie responds, warmly.

"She is. She's made me dream of things that I thought could only be imagined in fairytales, love songs, or daydreams. You know," Lee says more quietly so as not to draw more attention to himself from the other passengers, "I can't believe I'm on this flight, tonight. A little over two months ago I was ready to give up on dating for good and now look at me, sitting on a plane and confessing these things to a total stranger and not being embarrassed by it, at all. What do you say to that? It's a funny thing in a funny world."

Barbie nods her head and begins walking down the brightly lighted aisle. Lee settles back into his seat. Just as his eyes once again begin to close, Barbie startles him by unexpectedly tapping his shoulder. Before he has time to speak, she says, softly, "You know, I once heard of a man who loved a woman so much that he quite literally traveled around the world, from the US to Australia, just to buy her favorite brand of chocolate to present to her as he proposed. Isn't that something? What do you think of that?" she asks, rhetorically.

"I think," Lee says so quietly that Barbie almost doesn't hear, "That's The Way Love Goes."

CRY FOR ME

Cry for me.

Will you not cry for me?

Why do you not cry for me?

I have seen you cry for the brave, the bold, and the blundering who do nothing but blame you for their misdeeds.

I have seen you cry for the rancorous, the vicious, and the wicked who only seek to destroy you.

Often have I seen you cry for the rich, the famous, the beautiful, and the well-to-do.

Though rarely, I have even seen you cry for the downtrodden, the peacemaker, and the innocent.

You readily cry for yourself at each opportunity, be it self made or self-fulfilling, of which I do not know.

Cry for me.

Will you not cry for me?

Why do you not cry for me?

For me, it seems, you shed not a tear.

For me, you only shed vengeance, hatred, disgust, and despair.

For me, you ostentatiously exude darkness, repugnance, and detestation.

You are ghoulishly titillated, stimulated, and vindicated as my ever waning faith in you, in us, shatters into tiny shards of salty liquid glass as your contempt for me, your disdain of me erupts into viscerally-charged verbal mirrors of your soul.

Gaming me, feigning me, and ultimately blaming me is all you seem to know.

Cry for me.

Will you not cry for me?

Why do you not cry for me?

Have I not been there for you in your darkest hour?

Was I not there for you, ahead and beyond all others, when the tendrils of terror entwined your thoughts as you lay in the hospital bed?

When you called for me, in the midnight hour, did I not offer my weary arms as I stood up for you, stood up with you, and stood by you in the recovery lair?

When you cried, did I not cry with you?

Cry for me.

Will you not cry for me?

Why do you not cry for me?

After all I have done and attempted to do for you, for us, you glimpse me as a headmaster does a troublesome pupil, as a canine does a flea, as a vampire does the Holy cross; but there is nothing Holy about your commitment to me.

Emptiness, hopelessness, and powerlessness is all you wish me to see.

At best, you gaze upon me as though I were a nuisance, an annoyance, a dreary matinee.

Are there no tears for wandering, wondering, Candle Shore boys?

You court hypocrisy, embrace deception, and caress chaos with the enthusiasm of a young lover.

Yet, from me, you turn away.

I will cry for you, I promise.

I will remember all of the moments you thanked me for crying with you and your true family, of which I was never permitted to join.

I will remember the times when we, you and I, cried together with joy, with hope, with love.

On the last day, I will cry, just as I did on the first.

During our final moments, what remains of my broken heart will weep just as it does, right now.

Someday, and oh so late, you will come to know that I and only I, cried for you, thus, you were never alone.

And when I close my eyes for the last time, you will yet again not cry, for you will not know.

Cry for me.

Will you not cry for me?

Why did you not cry for me? my beloved wife.

EIGHTEEN HOURS

It's three a.m. when he opens his eyes and pushes forward and down on the footrest of the recliner that he's been dozing in for over two hours. A single nightlight is the only source of illumination in the tiny hospital room. He turns slightly in his chair and looks at the figure sleeping on the bed beside him.

After a few moments pass, he returns to his original position in the chair and begins thinking about the events of the past eighteen hours for he is quite certain that they have been the longest eighteen hours of his life. He thinks about how it is that he is in this hospital, sitting in this chair, beside this woman.

"You're just not the kind of man I want in my life, right now," she says indignantly. "Frankly," she continues, "you bore me to tears."

"I never used to bore you to tears," he retorts, sullenly. He knows he is reacting like an adolescent teenager but he can't help himself, this hurts. Her words bore deep holes into his soul and as a result, he can feel his confidence begin to drain away. "I used to be exactly what you wanted in a man or so you said."

A long silence is heard and felt between them.

"I've been seeing someone else," she says, so, so softly that it is almost a whisper.

Her words echo in his mind as he tries to rest in the recliner. The shock and the pain and the anger, even in this place and at this late hour, continues to consume and burn red-hot inside him. She stirs in her sleep. Her eyelids flutter. An expression of anguish crosses her face for an instant and then is gone.

"... Just get the hell out of my house, right now!" she yells. Her face is flushed with frustration and anger.

Opening the door, he says calmly but firmly, "I can't help it if I'm boring. I can't help it if I prefer oatmeal to omelets. I love you. What more do you want from me?"

"More than you could ever give me, I'm afraid."

But that had been over eighteen hours ago and now, here he is sitting beside her as she lay sleeping. Here he is sitting beside the one who had crushed his hopes and dreams. Here he is sitting beside the one who had cheated on him. Here he is sitting beside the one who had, just as he'd opened the front door of her house to leave, as she'd demanded, fallen to the floor as a result of a massive heart attack. Here he is sitting beside the woman who is now fighting for her life.

As his eyes begin to close, her voice, barely a whisper, rises up to him from the bed. "Is it you?" she asks.

"Yes," he says, sitting up and leaning forward in his chair, "it's me. I'm here."

"Do you hate me?"

"No, I could never hate you, not for long, anyway."

A small smile touches her lips. She says, eyes closed, "How can you stand to look at me after what I've done to us?"

"I don't know," he answers quietly, "it must be all of that oatmeal, I guess."

There is a long silence and then she asks, "How long will you stay?"

"For as long as you need me."

"How can you be so kind to me after what I've done?" she asks, truly perplexed.

As he hears himself reply to her question, he is struck by the awesome truth and power of what he is saying. "Because," he begins, "That's The Way Love Goes."

DEAD MAN'S RAP

Stay away, man, stay away. You don't want to come in here, believe me it's bad in here.

I'm telling you that things are just not right in this place and it's bad, I mean really bad in here and dark, like almost black, man.

I don't know how it started. I guess I just got curious, man; yeah, that's right, I got just a little too curious. Yeah man, I got a little too close, peeped inside one too many times, and forgot to walk away when I had the chance.

Now I'm inside it and it's inside me; baby, I'm locked and loaded with black flames frozen and there are no more chances for me.

Don't look, man and whatever you do, don't stare. Turn your eyes away while you still can. Get too close to this and you'll start to smell it and if you're not terribly careful you'll touch it and it'll touch you and then, man, and then, and then, it's on, baby; yeah, it'll really be on.

They say there used to be light in here and wind too; but those days are long gone, man, long, long gone. There's nothing in here but people like us, you know the type, right baby? All that's left in here is the funk of a lot of dark days and the stench of a lot of lightless nights. It's hot in here most of the time, hot, moist, and sticky, too.

Look too long and you'll get the hunger, man, just like me. You might just get trapped in this wet sticky stuff just like I did, oh yeah, just like me. You think you're too clever for that, don't you man? Yeah, I know you think you are; but you're wrong friend, you're deep down dirty dead wrong.

Hey! What are you doing? You're coming too close, man just like I did. It's awake now and it's going to touch you soon.

Ok, man, you want in? Is this really what you want? I know it seems like a funky filthy fantasy but the price is so high.

There are no walls in this place and there is no sky. There are no tomorrows in this world. There is only the never ending hunger of today. There is music but the music is bad; and all who enter this place must dance to the music throughout eternity, man. Do you understand me?

Maybe you'll be the one who finds a way out of here but I don't think so.

Oh no, you're too close, man. Ok, baby, you're all the way in, now. Do you feel it? Do you feel the gnawing insatiable hunger yet? You've got it now. Yeah, that's right, you've got it. Yeah, you've really got it bad. Does it feel good? Yeah I know it does at first, at least, only now it's time to begin. Yeah, man, It's time to begin the "DEAD MAN'S RAP."

THE ENDING

As he walks out of the house he knows that this will be the last time. He doesn't want it to be the last time, but the last, it is.

And she waits. There is pain in the waiting, pain and anxiety, too. She does not like waiting; for her, it is a test--a test that measures her indifference and her resolve. It is a test she cannot pass. As far as she is concerned, waiting is a watered-down form of torture--a torture without purpose, which, of course, makes her feel even more humiliated.

She waits for him--the man--the evil one. She knows, in her heart, that he is evil because he is so very good to her. She knows that he must be corrupt because he is just too kind, too generous, too caring and considerate. In short, he is everything she has ever wanted in a man; thus, he is too good to be true. Through her years, on this earth, she has learned that if something or someone seems too good to be true, then she, he or it probably is.

And she waits.

He paces back and forth along the deserted beach. He is whiling away the hours until it is time to see her again. He is nervous. He is always nervous when he thinks about being close to her--Hell, he gets the shakes just talking to her on the telephone. She is everything he has ever wanted in a woman--everything any man, human or otherwise, could--should ever want. She is too beautiful to touch. Sometimes he tries to convey these feelings to her but his tongue, inevitably, knots up into a child-like tangle of useless non-sequitous sentence fragments. He hates himself when this happens. He always feels stupid--like an imbecile. He hates himself for being just a man because a man, a mere mortal is not worthy of her affections. He simply feels that he does not possess a large enough vocabulary, if such a thing is possible, to express his eternal undying passion for her. Lately, he finds himself sitting behind his desk thinking about her. No matter how badly his day might be going thoughts of her always make him feel fine, very fine indeed.

She walks to the door. She thinks she heard something. Nothing, just the sound of some bird on the wind, perhaps. She goes back into the living room, sits on the sofa and begins to think. She thinks about him, the bad one--thinks about how he seduced her. She thinks about all of the cards and letters he sends telling of his overwhelming love for her. She thinks about the candle-lit dinners and the misty oil baths he gives her. She thinks about the look in his eyes when they are united in that perfect expression of trusting testament.

She rises from the sofa and walks over to the window and remembers how her life used to be before her romantic catalyst entered it. Before him, there had been no anxiety, no wanton desire. She had been happy with her life; it had been simple and complete. She had had her friends, her hobbies and her job to fulfill her life. She hadn't had to worry about anyone else's feelings or needs or problems. She hadn't had to consider what someone else might want for dinner or wonder where someone else might be at any given time. She hadn't had to concern herself with making compromises or concessions. In short, she hadn't had to answer to anyone and no one had to answer to her. God was in her heaven and all was right in her world. Then, he had come.

And she waits.

And he is in route to her home, now--enough stalling. It is time. He can't help feeling that something is going to go wrong this time. He thinks about his life before he met her. It was hard to imagine a time without her. His life had been, for the most part, rather satisfactory. He had been successful in his line of work and both little children and animals liked him very much. All things considered, he liked himself and his environment. He didn't think of himself as pure, inviolate, or anything so grandiose but he did think that he possessed enough redeeming qualities to, if not overlook his imperfections, at least, forgive them.

And then she had come and all things both good and bad dimmed before the glory of her beauty. In his heart of hearts he truly believed that he had never set his eyes upon such total grace, elegance and beauty. She was the icon of his every dream and desire. He remembered the way she had first regarded him. She had been kind but not overly friendly--sweet but not excessively jovial. And even though she knew how he felt about her, she never took his affection for granted.

In his life he had wanted, worked hard for and gotten many things but he knew, within moments of meeting her for the first time, that he would never want or work harder to have anyone as he was about to in the coming years of his life.

It was the right thing to do--the only thing to do. She couldn't let this continue--it just wouldn't be prudent. In another twenty minutes he would be at her door bearing some new gift, no doubt. She wondered what it would be this time, flowers, candies, a watch or a bracelet. She never knew what it would be but she did know that it would be.

The thing she couldn't understand was why he loved her, so. She did not consider herself ugly but she certainly did not have the extraordinary charm and beauty that he thought she had. Overall, she considered herself to be a slightly above average-looking woman. Sometimes, when he would look at her she could swear that he wasn't seeing her for what she was but rather, what he wanted her to be, an angel or something. She could not be with someone who would not--could not see her for what she really was, whatever that might be. She would ask him time and time again what it was that attracted him to her. He would respond with some silly answer like, "I think it's chemical." She did not like this answer because it left too many unanswered questions in its wake. Once, he told her that she should just let it be and enjoy his love for what it was. The idea of just letting anything be was, to say the least, totally unacceptable to her.

She wanted him to see her dark side--the evil side and so, she had tried to put that part of herself on display. In her own words, she had, quite simply, been the biggest bitch she could possibly be. She had gone out of her way to start arguments with him. She had taken issue with everything he held dear--things she, herself, didn't even care about. She had even hung up the phone on him, twice. Nothing seemed to diminish his feelings for her.

She understood that he was not unaware of what she was trying to do and she also knew that he knew that she knew that he knew. When she finally had asked him why he continued to put up with her outrageous behavior, he simply responded, "I'll pass every test you give me, Honey. My love for you is not based on your actions but on your character."

She knew that it was just a matter of time before he would show his true colors--just a matter of time.

She waits.

Her words ring in his head, "You are too involved with me. I don't know if I want a relationship like this, yet or if I ever will. You are trying to take control of my life and I don't like it." Her words make him angry--make him hate her for an instant. It has been said that there is a thin line between love and hate and that that line can be crossed in the blink of an eye. He wonders why she is so stubborn and unyielding. He feels like, in a way, he is being toyed with--pacified, from time to time, like an infant. This thought humiliates and enrages him and he thinks, just for a moment, that he should say to her, "To Hell with you--you stupid bitch!"

He remembers a time, earlier in his life, when he would have had the strength to walk away but that time has long since passed. He has become soft, week, complacent. He remembers the time when fire burned in his eyes and in his heart--a fire that could, once upon a time, have burned the perditions throne right out from beneath the devil, himself.

"I am a man," he whispers to himself, "and I can't believe I am letting that woman treat me like this." Immediately after saying this he begins to feel ashamed. He tells himself that he isn't being fair to her. He whispers, "Some people just need more time." He is beginning to feel tired, though, very tired indeed. What is he to do? He doesn't want to scare her away and yet he doesn't want to spend the rest of his life wanting someone he cannot have. There must be fairness, somewhere-- some day.

He is feeling weary, now. He, almost, doesn't look forward to seeing her, today. Talking to her is like an exercise in discipline--in caution. When they talk, either in person or on the phone, his stomach becomes a sack of hot liquid lava and his head, a dome of agonizing uncertainty. In short, conversing with her is, more often than not, horrible. He wonders if he will walk away from her and never return. In the far reaches of his soul, he knows that he may have to face that possibility, some day. This makes him profoundly sad.

He is getting closer, now. He is getting closer to her not only in proximity but also in the truth. Truth can be a very painful thing. It can hurt--sting--cut like a knife--and it never, ever bends, not even for a king. He knows that he loves her--loves her more than anyone else in the world but he also knows that he can not sacrifice his life for her--to her. Their existence together could be-- should be very simple. He wants her and she, him; nothing could be simpler.

She worries about so many things that cannot be resolved by any one action or any one revelation. Why couldn't she just enjoy their time together and work to achieve a more gentle balance between the reality of their needs and the validity of their passions in the distance.

He sees her house.

He walks to the front door and stops. He cannot move.

She knows he is there even before he knocks on the door--she knows it and abhors it.

They walk into the parlor in silence. They sit, side-by-side, on the sofa. They look into each other's eyes. She touches his hand and he begins to cry. She leans forward and kisses his tears. He cannot speak. She too, can find no words to speak. She sees the look on his face and, for the first time, sees him for what he really is, a man in love. She is scared of him no longer..

They kiss; for you see, "That's the way love goes."

LETTER:
There Is Light In The Dark

Please, please do not be embarrassed by your dilemma, my friend.

Believe me, I understand.

Many, many moons ago when I first arrived in Candle Shore, I, quite simply, ran out of money.

In order to survive, I had to go to work at the food bank in order to receive payment in the form of government food, once a week.

For the first time in my life I found myself working beside ex-cons, prostitutes, and parolees who wanted to do anything but be there. They were very angry people. I discovered, to my amazement, that some of these people carried weapons and would not hesitate to use them on anyone, if they so chose.

One day, I'll never forget it, I was taking a break from loading a truck, when someone decided to take the candy bar, I was preparing to eat, out of my hand. It was one of the prostitutes. She reached up and before I could stop her, grabbed it and ran just out of my field of vision which was about five feet. She started giggling as she tore off the paper and began to eat. I honestly thought someone, for there were several witnesses, would help me protest but no one did. They just stood around and laughed at me. I was so hungry that day and that candy bar was all the food I would have to eat for the next six hours.

I was angry and heart broken. I suppose my anger began to show in my demeanor for the next thing I knew was that one of her "friends", smelling of urine, put a knife to the back of my neck and said, "You ain't gonna get an attitude, are you, blind boy?"

Tears came to my eyes as I shook my head. Then he said, "I'm sure she'll pay you back, if you know what I mean, if you'd like. Want me to talk to her for you?"

I was absolutely disgusted and shyly declined his offer.

As I returned to my work, I remember thinking, "How did this happen? How did I end up in this place? All this and for what, some food?"

The tears did not go away, at least, not that day.

The most horrible thing is that I could not tell any of my friends that I was having financial problems. I did not want to hear any lectures from them and I know that my family was just waiting for me to fail. They, believe me, never thought I could survive out here in Candle Shore without their benevolent help.

You know, I remember feeling so much like a loser because, while my friends were going out on dates with girls, I was sitting home, eating government cheese, and hoping I would not feel the tiny feet of roaches cross my legs, again.

I had to sell many things in order to keep the electricity and telephone on. In those days, I only had one plate, two forks, two spoons, one cutting knife, two butter knives, one frying pan with no lid, one pot with lid, two cereal bowls, two cups, two glasses, one water pitcher, one canopener, four saucers, and one serving spoon.

How can I remember this list of items so clearly after all these years?

I can remember because I coveted them so. Aside from my already outdated desktop computer, a small television set, some second hand clothes, various sundry items, and a few pieces of much used furniture, it was all I owned in the world.

It seems so long ago, now; almost as if it all happened to someone else but it did not, it happened to me; or, more precisely, I happened to it.

I know that my words will not ease your pain but I do hope that they illustrate that you have absolutely nothing of which to be ashamed; just don't give up and, more importantly, don't give into anything or anyone who does not believe in you.

Beware your friends for they may be blinded by love. Covet your enemies for it is your reaction to your enemies through which your true self will be revealed.

Hear my words in your heart and you will soon discover that there is light in the dark.

THE CYCLE

She hates waiting for the water to drain out of the bathtub. She feels like an absolute fool just sitting there watching the rusty mouth of the drain slowly and loudly gulp down her murky grey and now cold bathwater, between her old, tired, and very, very wrinkled feet. She's starting to get chilly, now.

She always waits for the water to drain before attempting to exit the tub. Last year she had not waited, against her doctor's recommendation and as a result, she had fallen back into the tub badly bruising the entire left side of her body. It had taken months to recover. The mere thought of the pain still makes her wince.

She manages to squeeze out a place to sit on the narrow bench at the bus shelter by forcing herself down between two burley men. Both men have distinctively different but equally offensive body odors. The man on her left smells as though he has not taken a bath in over a month and she can tell that the man on her right has recently vomited on himself.

It's raining and all the would-be passengers are desperately trying to stay dry by shoving, jamming, or pushing themselves into the obscenely small shelter. She wishes that she did not have to try to stay dry by having to sit between these two filthy people. If only her umbrella had not been snatched away by that prostitute as she made her way to the bus stop today.

Now here she is, sitting on a wet bench. Cold water soaks her clothing all the way through to her under garments. An icy wet chill makes its way up her spine.

To the extreme left end of the shelter there are two young girls playing a radio much too loudly and to the extreme right, there is a homeless man praying to himself and rubbing his right arm with his left hand which, she notices, is covered in grimy soot. He looks as though he spent the night in a dumpster.

Two more people squeeze onto the bench. She is being pressed hard from both sides and she is finding it very difficult to breathe. The man on her immediate right sneezes and does not bother to cover his nose. Some of his expulsion lands on her knee. She grimaces.

Finally, the bus arrives and she and her fellow bus riders stand and prepare to board. She tries to get close to the bus but she is being pushed back and walked in front of by these people. They all push in front of her and she is the last to get on. As she pays her fare, the bus driver, looking very impatient, growls "Hang on lady." She frantically looks for any empty seats but they have all been taken. The bus jerks forward. She falls.

As her husband closes the door behind himself as he leaves for work in the coalmines, the young eighteen year old woman breathes a sigh of relief. She hadn't known how he would respond when she told him she was pregnant. She had heard that many men got really angry at the thought of trying to raise a family these days since the stock market crash, last year in 1929.

She'd always wanted children but now that things were so bad she was not sure if she and her husband of eleven months could stand the financial strain of raising a family. She recalls how his facial expression had not changed during their short two minute conversation. He had remained calm upon hearing the news and the only thing he'd said in response was, "Well, I've got to get to the mines."

She's home now, finally. The old woman sits in her easy chair racked with pain from her fall on the bus which had occurred exactly one week ago today. She had broken her left arm and two ribs as well as her left collarbone.

She's home now, alone.

The bus company had quickly offered her an enormous amount of money in compensation for her, as the bus company attorneys had put it, "little tumble" and she had promptly accepted. Upon signing the forms that released the bus company from any and all legal responsibility for her "little tumble", she'd realized that money, for the first time in her long, long life, would no longer be a problem.

She's alone now, tired--tired of her life and tired of living. She's alone in the world now. Everyone and anyone who had ever mattered to her has long since passed away including her beloved husband of fifty years and her one and only daughter.

As she sits in her favorite chair waiting for the soothing balm of the pain medication to wash over her for the last time, she wonders who, if anyone, will miss her. Probably no one, she concludes.

It's raining today, just like it was on the day of her fall. She listens to the sound of it hitting the rooftop; it sounds like little tiny rolling marbles. It's a soothing sound, a nostalgic sound, a peaceful sound. She's glad it's raining today, her last day.

Today--today, today. "Is there something about today?" she asks herself. Oh yes. Today is her birthday, she remembers.

A very sad and lonely old woman sits in her favorite easy chair, alone, thinking, and softly weeping on her birthday.

"What's wrong!" the woman exclaims, eyes squinted shut and jaws clinched tight with pain.

"I'm not sure, honey" the woman's mother replies, nervously. "The baby's not moving down like it's supposed to. I've never seen this before."

"Oh God!" the woman on the bed says in a breathless staccato. "Oh God--this can't be happening," she adds, tears streaming down her face.

The young woman on the bed in a darkened room of a little wooden house has been in labor for over ten hours now. When it had become apparent that it was time for her to deliver, her mother had gone next door to a neighbor and asked one of the children to go find a nurse or a doctor. At the onset of labor all had gone as expected for awhile but now, now something was terribly wrong.

"Mama, what's gonna happen?"

The crying woman's mother looks down at her one and only daughter, brushes her hair away from her sweaty brow with her left hand and replies in a whisper, "I surely don't know."

The long anticipated balmy soothing wave of unconsciousness finally reaches the old woman sitting in her chair and engulfs her and, at last, her wait is over.

Blackness follows.

Blackness--nothing but blackness and, strangely enough, blackness sprinkled with consciousness. Strange--it's not supposed to be this way, is it? A feeling of gently spinning in the blackness, which is slowly, ever so slowly becoming dark grey, crosses the threshold of her awareness.

Is this the way it's supposed to be? She wonders. Is this death? The dark grey has now become light grey. The spinning sensation becomes more and more intense.

"Hey lady," a young voice says from above her.

She is lying on her back, apparently on wet grass, with her eyes closed. She feels raindrops falling on her face. The wind is blowing and it's cold out here.

"Hey lady," the young voice repeats, "are you alright?"

She opens her eyes and sees the owner of the voice. He is a young boy approximately fourteen years old or so. "I'm alright," she finally answers, somewhat bewildered. "Just help me up, young man."

The boy reaches down and takes her right hand. She raises herself up from the wet grass.

As she gets to her feet, pain envelops her, once again. "Am I dead?" she asks herself. "Is this a dream?" She wonders. No, she reasons, this cannot be death or a dream because the pain is much too sharp and too specific to the bruised areas of her old body.

Looking sternly at the boy, she asks, "Where am I, young man?" The boy, looking somewhat befuddled, says, "Why, you're in Candle Shore, Ma'am." He adds, "You're gonna get really wet if you don't get inside." Upon saying this, the young man removes his hooded yellow rain jacket and offers it to her. She gladly accepts.

"Did you faint or something?"

While putting on the rain jacket and bringing up the hood around her face she replies softly, "No, I don't think so. The last thing I remember is sitting in my chair in my home in Madisonville."

The boy's hair is getting soaked from the rain. "Well," he begins, "I don't know where Madisonville is but you're in Candle Shore now."

"I'll walk you somewhere so you won't get wet and then I've got to find a nurse or a doctor or someone." He glances about in order to demonstrate his urgency.

The old woman, noticing the strained and tense look on the young man's flat oval shaped face says, "Are you ill?"

"No. A neighbor is having a baby and she needs help," he answers.

"I used to be a nurse. Perhaps I can help your neighbor." The boy's face lights up as he realizes that he has successfully completed his task. Eyes widened with a flame of hope, the boy says eagerly, "Yes Ma'am. That's great. This way--let's go."

They begin to walk.

"We're almost there, Ma'am," the boy says to her as they make their way down an unpaved and now muddy road. The boy notices that his companion is starting to walk slower and breathe harder. "Are you OK?" he asks.

"Yes, I'm fine son--just keep going, I'll make it."

They've been walking in silence for the past fifteen minutes, making their way in the now pouring rain. As they walk, the old lady ponders about how she came to be in this place. One minute she had been sitting in her warm comfortable familiar easy chair waiting for ... and the next, lying outside on wet grass in the rain. Where had the boy said she was? Oh yes, Candle Shore. "Candle Shore," she thinks to herself as she walks. Where had she heard that name before? The name tickles a distant memory in her mind but, like so many others these days, it remains beyond her grasp of recollection.

"OK," the boy's voice stops her train of thought.

"What was that, boy?" she asks.

"OK," he repeats, "we're here."

She and the boy are standing in front of a small wooden house. "We can just go in," he informs her.

They walk up three steps and onto the front porch. As the young man turns the weather-worn knob and opens the front door, the old woman feels a sudden tightening in her chest just above her heart. She clutches her bosom and falls forward into the house.

She's awakened by the sound of a man's voice saying, "I think she's going to be alright. It's a good thing I got here when I did." The old woman opens her eyes to see a slightly older than middle-aged man looking down at her. She is lying on a couch in the front room of the house that no doubt belongs to the door that her young companion had opened just before she fainted.

Seeing that she has regained consciousness, the man says to her, "You gave us quite a scare. How do you feel?"

Quickly trying to gather her thoughts she replies "OK I guess. I don't know, really." She looks around the room and sees the young boy who had guided her to this place. He's sitting beside a young girl who, judging by her flat oval-shaped face, must be his sister.

"Doctor," a woman yells from the next room, "please come back in here--my daughter's bleeding badly." The man turns and walks into the next room.

The young boy stands and walks over to the old woman and says, looking back towards the young girl, "That's my sister. She's the one who found the doctor." The old woman smiles at the sullen faced child sitting quietly across the room.

Returning her gaze back to the boy she says while straining to stand up, "Well, help me up. I came here to help and that's what I'm going to do." The young man complies. She walks towards the doorway that leads to the bedroom where the pregnant woman, the pregnant woman's mother, and the doctor are.

As she approaches the doorway she hears a woman ask nervously, "Doctor, what's going to happen to my daughter and the baby?" The doctor does not immediately answer.

Then, "I believe the baby is going to be just fine but I'm afraid I cannot save your daughter. She's hemorrhaging deep from within and I cannot stop it. I'm so sorry Mrs. …"

As she hears the woman's name, that tickle of a memory in the back of her mind becomes a ferocious itch. That name sounds familiar to her, so very familiar.

Then, like a pane of glass shattering in her mind, the fragments of recollection fall into place and she remembers.

Once, many, many years ago when she still lived in the orphanage, she had asked to see her birth records. She must have been about thirteen years old. The orphanage's records keeper had initially resisted showing her the files for fear that they may upset her; but the persistent child had cried, whined, and pleaded until the bewildered records keeper gave into her request.

During her review of the files she learned that her mother had died while giving birth to her. She learned that her grandmother, apparently her only living relative at the time, had died three months after her birth. While her father's name had been listed on her birth certificate, there had been a scribbled note in the upper left-hand corner of the document which read, "Father dead due to mining accident." The records listed her place of birth as Candle Shore.

The old woman turns away from the bedroom and returns to the couch.

"How can this be?" she whispers to herself. "Please God, tell me--how is this possible?"

The two children look across the room at her with sad expressions on their faces. She realizes that they must think she's referring to the event taking place in the next room. She knows that they have no idea of what she is really questioning.

For as long as she could remember, she had always wanted to meet her mother--to touch her mother--and to ask her questions. She remembers how her perspective on life had abruptly changed after seeing those orphanage files. From that day on, she had felt guilty about being alive because her life had killed her own mother. It had been on that day that she started hating herself and resenting other children who, forever unlike herself, would grow up with their parents.

Sitting on the couch, the old woman recalls how from the moment of seeing those records at the age of thirteen until well into her twenties, her life had dramatically changed for the worst in ways that she couldn't even bare to think about anymore. It had been a miracle that she'd made it through those dark days.

A shrill cry from the other room jolts her back into the present. "That's my mama in there," she thinks to herself as she stands and walks, once again, towards the bedroom.

Afraid to step all the way in, the old woman stops at the threshold which is located at the foot of a bed upon which a young woman is lying. The young woman on the bed has just given birth. Although the lower half of her body has been covered with blankets, the old woman can see blood starting to seep through the fabric eerily bathing them in a dark crimson red. Standing on the right side of the bed is the doctor touching the woman's left upper arm. Standing to the left of the bed, is the young woman's mother holding a tiny baby in her arms. The old woman, still standing in the doorway, is overcome with grief and sadness. She looks at the young woman's face and sees that fear, sorrow, fatigue, and above all else, pain has settled over the new mother's simple yet pleasant features. She is only half conscious now--drained from the fatal process of giving life to her daughter.

The child begins to cry. At the sound of her baby, the young woman looks towards her mother and says, "Is she OK? Is she going to be OK?"

The baby's grandmother looks across the bed to the doctor who answers reassuringly, "She's going to be just fine. She's a beautiful healthy baby girl."

Blood continues to creep across the bottom half of the woman and the bed like a river of ruby colored molasses. The old woman can smell it from where she stands; the unmistakable odor of wet copper.

"Let me hold her. I want to hold my baby." The new mother slowly and very weakly raises her arms towards the crying infant. The baby's grandmother gently lowers the precious package into her mother's waiting arms. The infant's cries subside almost immediately.

"OH God." She tries to raise her head in order to see her baby better but she is too weak.

"I'm so tired, Mama," the young woman says to her mother.

"I know you are, baby. You did a good job today; you gave me a grandbaby today. It's been a long day for you. Try to rest now. I'll take the baby and clean her up for you." She reaches down to take the baby girl but the new mother resists saying, "No, I don't have much time left and I want to be with my daughter for as long as I can, Mama, please."

The child's grandmother stops reaching for the baby, lowers her head, and begins sobbing silently. The doctor pulls up a chair next to the bed and sits. There are tears in his eyes.

The young woman's eyes begin to close. She says in almost a whisper, "Tell her I love her. Tell her that I love her so much. Tell her that the best thing I ever did in my life was to give birth to her. Tell her that I love her so much that it hurts, Mama. Tell her that my love will always be with ..." her voice trails off.

The old woman who has been completely silent steps forward into the room and says with tears in her eyes and a quiver in her voice, "Mama, I'm here. I hear you."

Both the grandmother and the doctor look up in surprise at the sound of the old woman's voice. The young woman slowly opens her eyes trying to locate the source of the new voice in the room. She looks down towards the foot of her bed and sees a figure standing there.

The old woman and the young mother make eye contact for just one brief fleeting moment and then the young woman's eyes close, never to open again.

The old woman falls to the floor of the bedroom, unconscious.

Blackness, stillness, and silence.

The old woman opens her eyes to the familiar surroundings of her home in Madisonville. Rain is still pounding the roof of her house. She is sitting in her warm and comfortable favorite easy chair. She looks down her front and sees that she has vomited on herself. "I must have thrown up the pills," she thinks, remembering that the book had instructed that one should thoroughly crush the tablets and mix them with liquid before ingesting. She had forgotten to do this and as a result, here she is, still alive.

She reflects on what she has just witnessed. "My God," she whispers in the stillness. Had she really been there in the same room with her very own mother, grandmother, and herself? Her mind reels at the thought. "It just couldn't have been a dream--it just couldn't have been," she resolves.

The woman she had seen on the bed hadn't looked at all like the woman in her dreams. For some unknown reason, she had always envisioned her mother as a short-haired, slightly overweight, below-average looking working-class woman of her day. The woman she had seen on the bed, however, had been absolutely beautiful with long flowing hair, smooth features, and deep sincere eyes.

Sitting once again in her bathtub, the old woman hears her mother's last words in her mind, "Tell her I love her. Tell her that I love her so much. Tell her that the best thing I ever did in my life was to give birth to her. Tell her that I love her so much that it hurts, Mama. Tell her that my love will always be with ..."

"Me," the old woman says, out loud, completing her mother's last thought.

As she remembers her mother's words, she begins thinking about some of the past events of her life. During those early years, when things had really been bad, she'd sometimes felt as though someone was watching over her. She remembers that time in the alley when that man had tried to rape her. She remembers that, as he got on top of her, she had suddenly felt an unexplainable and yet undeniable burst of energy giving her the strength to push him off before he had a chance to commence his dirty business. She remembers how so many times, during the course of her long life when seemingly all had been lost, a miraculous turn of events had been waiting for her just around the proverbial corner. Several times during those early years she had tried to commit suicide without success. She remembers that time when her pistol had misfired twice during what she then thought would be her final attempt. After that, things had gotten better, much better. At the age of 30 she met a man--a very good man, fell in love, and married him. She, like her mother, had given birth to only one child, a daughter who became the joy of her life.

Sitting in her bathtub once again watching the rusty mouth of the drain slowly and loudly gulp down her murky grey and now cold bathwater, she remembers how she had wanted to be there for her baby, always.

She had wanted her child to have a mother--the best mother in the world, and according to her late daughter, she had succeeded.

And now, thanks to her "little tumble" on the bus, money would never again be a problem.

Had all of these good things happened to her because of her deceased mother's love? All those sleepless nights, in those early years when she'd felt as though she were being watched, had that been her mom?

She stares at her tired old feet and smiles because, for some reason, they don't look so wrinkled today.

"I'm going to take a trip around the world," she says out loud as the last of the water drains from the tub. "There's an entire world out there I've never seen and I want to see it, for my mom."

Heeding her doctor's recommendation, she carefully steps out of the tub.

"Tell her I love her. Tell her that I love her so much. Tell her that the best thing I ever did in my life was to give birth to her. Tell her that I love her so much that it hurts, Mama. Tell her that my love will always be with ..."

The old woman thinks about her own deceased daughter and in so doing realizes how strong a mother's love can be. She knows, in her heart of hearts, that not even death can keep her love from her sweet baby because, quite simply, "That's The Way Love Goes."

TO MY DREAMER

My Dreamer:

The gift I gave you and will give to you again and again was born from the warmth and sincerity of my love.

Fancy it and, alas, fancy me; for you are my one true sweet, sly, silly, sultry and seasoned dreamer of old.

Let my gift embrace your dreams and let its fire ignite the flight that will ferry your thoughts to where they wish to go.

Ease your mind into the mist of my gift, close your eyes, and think of me.

Rest your dark essence upon my immortal hopes and primordial desires; and dream. Dream of who you are, who I am, and what we will become, together.

Until we met, I dared not ponder the wonders of the universe nor peer too closely into the shadows of my soul; but then you came unto me and I, to you, and the candles of my own dreams began to glow.

Accept my gift, my beloved dreamer and trust that, as one, we shall never let the dream, the one and only beautiful dream, erode.

A TRIP TO VAULDEN

As she picks up the telephone receiver she knows whose voice she will hear on the other end of the line. She knows and yet she answers anyway. As the cold plastic touches her ear she hears him begin to speak.

"Hello?"

She replies with dread in her voice, "Hello--what do you want now?"

"Hi I'm glad I didn't get your voicemail, again--I absolutely hate that thing."

"Yes--I know you do. Is something wrong or are you just calling to bother me again."

"Why must you say things like that--ever since you got married you've been different--did you know that?"

She screws up her face in frustration. He always managed to say the most stupid and blatantly obvious things to her.

After a short pause she answers, "Of course I know that. Marriage, a good marriage anyway, does that to you. If he knew I was accepting calls from you he would be very angry and probably start to hate me for it. This is not right--we should not be talking like this--I'm a married woman now."

"I know but there is nothing wrong with it--really--I mean, it's not like we're doing anything or anything."

Determined to either get an answer from him as to why he called or get him off the phone, she asks quite harshly, "What do you want?"

A short silence follows.

Then, finally, he says in a somewhat lower and less confident tone than before, "Well, I need your help."

She can tell by the sudden change in his demeanor that he lowered his head as he spoke those words. How well she knows him.

He continues, "I need you to take me to Vaulden."

"What? That's over a hundred miles away--across the state line. You can't be serious."

His words come fast and earnest, "Please! It's important--there's something I have to do, there. It's really important--please."

No answer for a very, very, very long time.

As she seats herself behind the steering wheel of her car she knows deep down that the day will soon come when she will regret having driven him to Vaulden; she knows this and yet, she turns the key in the ignition, backs out of her driveway, and points her car in the direction of his apartment located on the other side of the city.

Thank goodness her husband had to work out of town today, she thinks to herself as she drives across town. She wonders why she keeps letting this man exist in her world. They had not dated in over two years--hadn't lived together in over four.

Shortly after returning from her honeymoon she had introduced him to her husband. "Boy!" she says to herself, stopping at a red light. What a mistake that had been.

Although her husband clearly disapproved of her relationship with him, he had never said as much. Nevertheless, she knew that it was only a matter of time before he would make a very obvious request of her.

Since her marriage, it had always been her intention to end her now platonic relationship with him; and end it she would, before her husband came to her and rightly demanded as much. This--this trip to Vaulden would be the absolute last favor --last anything she would ever do for him. After all she was a married woman now and she wanted to move on with her life and that is exactly what she was going to do, period.

As she drives up next to him, standing on the curb, she knows that this will be the proverbial final scene in their little play.

And time passes.

The rain falls hard on her head as she waits for the bus to arrive. She holds an old piece of plastic over her head to defend against the rain but, like so many other things in her life these days, the rain is a formidable opponent. The water finds its way to her skull and she shivers; oh how she shivers. She waits for the bus.

Now seated on board, staring through one of the bus's deep dark green tinted windows, bound for Vaulden, she wonders--wonders what he will look like now. She has not seen his face in over fifteen years--hasn't even spoken to him in over twelve. Fifteen years, she thinks to herself, where did they go; fifteen years, she doesn't know. She sits on the bus to Vaulden and just wonders where they've gone.

The bus glides smoothly on to the freeway. "No turning back now," she says under her breath, "no turning back."

She had been so mean to him on that last day--the day when she had driven him across this exact same road to Vaulden. In the car, she had told him that she simply didn't have enough room in her life or in her heart for him, any longer; and that if he truly loved her as he tirelessly proclaimed he would go away and, more importantly, stay away for good and all. As she had said these things to him she could almost hear his heart break.

Upon their arrival in Vaulden, he had directed her to a rather large office building down on Main Street. Preparing to exit the car he had said, "Thank you so much. Wait here. This won't take long. I'll be back shortly." With that, he had leaned across and kissed her smartly on the cheek, opened the door, stepped out and turned and walked towards the building. She, however, had not waited for him. She, in fact, after seeing him disappear into the building, had simply driven away.

That had happened so long ago. Now here she was on her way to see a man whom she had left stranded in a city over one hundred miles away from his home.

Halfway there, now.

She's on the bus; staring through the window into the deep dark green milky universe, thinking.

Even before her husband's death, her life had begun to slowly and steadily spiral down into the very depths of misery.

Since his death, she had spent virtually all of their life's savings on their two children's court costs. It seemed that both of them had been in trouble with the law since the day they were born. Now she is living in a homeless shelter and she doesn't even know where her two children are these days.

A freeway sign reads, "Next Exit Vaulden."

She has walked two miles now; two miles from the bus stop. She stops in front of his house, a large beautiful two story home built on a meticulously manicured lawn. In her pocket are three quarters. As she slowly approaches the beautifully handcrafted mahogany double front doors, her tiny undernourished fingers curl around the coins like a drowning person's fingers might curl around a useless piece of driftwood from a sinking ship.

She rings the doorbell.

He answers.

Silence.

"My wife will be back soon."

"I see," she replies. They are sitting next to each other on a very comfortable sofa.

He continues, "She is going to wonder who you are and how I know you."

"Yes, I guess she will."

She tries to read his expression but, alas, after all these years she can no longer peek into his soul. He is a mystery to her, now.

"Well," he asks, "what do you want?"

She lowers her head and says, softly, "I need your help-- I really need your help, please."

Silence.

Time passes.

"Did you know my father, well?"

"Yes, I did," she replies. She is driving a very nice luxury car down the freeway to Vaulden. In the passenger seat of the vehicle sits a young teenage girl, teary-eyed, sad, and afraid.

She continues, "I knew your mother, as well, but I knew your father long before he met and married her. He and I used to be very good friends, once upon a time and many moons ago. It seems as though your dad and I have always found ourselves falling into and out of each other's lives over the years. Life can be funny that way, I suppose, if you're lucky."

The young girl asks, "How did it, the accident I mean, how did it happen?"

"I'm not sure," she answers honestly, "I'm really not sure at all."

The young girl begins to cry, quietly. Then she says, more to herself than to the woman beside her, "I was just lying in bed, in my dorm room, when the phone rang and...."

The young girl looks directly at the woman driving the car--looks for the very first time and says, rather uncomfortably, "I have no one, now--no one at all."

The car passes under a sign that reads, "Welcome To Vaulden."

While slowing down at the bottom of the off-ramp and then turning on to Candle Shore Lane, the woman says, "You have me honey; you will always have me. Your parents and I agreed long ago that if anything should happen to them I would take care of you."

The girl asks, truly puzzled, "Why you?"

The woman thinks about how to respond to this question as she parks the car in the driveway. They sit in the car, neither wanting to exit the vehicle until this question has been answered.

The woman knows that what she is about to say will be difficult for the child to understand--knows this and yet what must be said must be said.

The woman answers with calm deliberation saying, "Because when it's all said and done, quite simply, I was always there for your father when he needed me and he was always there for me when I needed him. Your dad and I may have lost touch with each other in the three dimensional world, throughout our lives, but we never lost touch in the infinite dimensions of our hearts. When

you really love someone, time and distance are
irrelevant. Love knows no boundaries.

"Your mother was enlightened enough to realize that a
man and a woman can love without lust. She was
gracious enough to allow your father to help me when I
needed help. Your mother's love for your father and
your father's love for me is the reason why I will always
take care of you. That's The Way Loves Goes."

LETTER:
To My Guardian Angel (2)

I want you to know that you are always in my heart and in my thoughts and I miss you so terribly much.

And I wish we could spend more time together for when we are together, time has no meaning and life, no limits.

The connection, the bond that we have is worth more to me than the finest treasures of my wildest dreams for dreams cannot bring me what you give to me in every thought of you, hope, joy, and peace.

I cannot explain it and, to be honest, I do not want to tame it. I only want to have it for the rest of my life.

I know how I feel about you and I trust how you feel about me.

Why?

Why, indeed; because the respect and grace you bestow upon me takes me to a higher level, takes me to a different plane of existence, takes me to where I thought I would never go and could never belong.

I truly wonder why God allowed you to fly to me at this point in my life for if we had met in the morning years, perhaps we could have traveled together.

Would we have gone together? Would your wings have touched mine?

Or were we always destined to share a distance, me a reflection of you and you, of me?

Do not harden at my questions for they are not meant to torment you but, rather, to convince you of how I love you so. For you are my angel and angels need to know.

THE WITNESS

(Bang--Bang-Bang!
The courtroom falls
silent as the judge
slams his gavel down.)

(Judge)   "Please answer the
question."

(The defendant closes
her eyes and then
opens them. She
lowers her head
slightly.)

(Defendant)   "I don't know--I guess I
was."

(The prosecutor
continues to pace back
and forth, back and
forth as he speaks.)

(Prosecutor)   "So then you admit that
you were there? Say it
again, louder, so
everyone can hear you.
So, you freely admit that
you were there?"

(The defense attorney
stands abruptly.)

(Defense)   "Objection, Your Honor!
Asked and answered!"

(Judge)   "Sustained."

(The defense attorney slowly returns to his seat satisfied with the result. The prosecutor stops directly in front of the somewhat slumped and shaken young lady sitting in the witness chair. He stares into her reddened eyes which are once again filling with tears of sorrow. His voice increases in volume and intensity with every word he speaks.)

(Prosecutor)   "Then how could you sit there and watch your own mother do that to herself? How could you be there and yet do nothing to stop her?"

(The defendant sits up straight in the witness chair, clearly surprised by the attack. She looks sharply at her interrogator. After a moment she turns her tear-soaked and now bewildered face towards the jury. With a hint of anger and impatience in her voice she speaks.)

(Defendant)   "I didn't! I tried to stop her--my hand grabbed hers just before she..."

(The prosecutor's voice softens.)

(Prosecutor) "Just before she what?"

(She speaks slowly and softly as an air of calmness settles over her.)

(Defendant) "When my hand grabbed hers she looked up at me. She didn't say anything; she just looked up at me. I'll never forget that look, that silence, that moment in time. I said, "Mom, I can't let you do this. I can't live without you.""

(The prosecutor urges her on, gently now.)

(Prosecutor) "Go on."

(Defendant) "She said, "Boopy, I don't want to live this way and if you really love me then please don't make me." Then she told me to lean down towards her and I did. She kissed me on my right eyelid--just like she used to do whenever I was scared or sad. She said, "Boopy, I want you to remember that mouse you used to have when

82

you were a little girl. Do
you remember?" I
remembered, and then,
I let go of her hand."

(Turning his gaze towards the jury box,
the prosecutor addresses its residents in
a flat businesslike manner.)

(Prosecutor)   "Let the record show
that "Boopy" was a
nickname used by the
defendant's mother as a
term of endearment.

(Returning his attention
to the defendant, he
speaks in a much lighter
and less intense tone
than before.)

(Prosecutor)   "What did she mean by
"that little mouse you
used to have"?"

(The air inside the tiny
courtroom is charged
with anticipation.
Everyone, jurors,
reporters, and
spectators alike, is
leaning forward to hear;
even the judge finds
himself caught up in her
words.)

(Defendant)   "She was reminding me
of a decision I had to
make many years ago
when I discovered that
my pet mouse, Casey,
whom I loved so dearly,

had broken all four of
his little legs. She was
reminding me that
sometimes, sometimes
all of us, little girls and
adults alike, have to do
things they don't want to
do, because..."

(Prosecutor)   "Because what?"

(She looks up towards
the ceiling, takes a deep
dark soul-shaking
breath and sighs.)

(Defendant)   "Because, when it's all said and done,
that's the way love goes."

THE PASSING

It's hard to believe it happened, now, but it did. I know. I was there. It's funny how the mind can forget so many things, funny. But, even at my old age, after all these years, I can still see her as clear as a bell.

I remember how she looked. She was the loveliest creation I had ever seen. Even though I was a young man with many years ahead of me, I knew that I would never set eyes on anything as beautiful as her, ever again. After all these years, I still feel that way. Sometimes I would walk down to the docks and look out over the water and see her sitting there, like an imperial queen sitting on a liquid throne of blue. Her name was Blue-Night. She was a deep dark navy-blue sailing vessel with white trim. As I would stand there, at the edge of the ocean, I would dream of the time when she and I would be together on the sea.

I'll never forget the day we set sail on the high sea. I'll tell you something, friend, there is not a greater more exhilarating experience for a young man than when he stands shoulder-to-shoulder with his shipmates, on a vessel built and bound for adventure, moving away from all that is familiar, to conquer the great unknown. I don't remember where we were going but I guess that's not important, anymore, we never got there. No sir, where we got to is what I'm going to tell you about.

It had been a clear day and the sun was shining, brightly. All hands were on deck as we departed and all of us, captain and midshipmen alike, were feeling fine, mighty fine. I remember seeing my Sally standing at the edge of the docks, a little ways from everybody else. I could see the sunlight reflecting off of her tears. One of my mates who, I guess, had been watching me watching her, put his hand on my shoulder and said, "It'll be alright, Mate, you'll be see'n her again real soon--and, you'll have a lot of money to spend on her, too." The captain gave the command and away we went.

Have you ever known the smells of a new ship? I do believe they're just about the best smells in the world. When I was not on duty, instead of reading some book or playing cards with the other fellows, I would walk around the ship--listening to her, smelling her--touching and becoming one with her. I see you smirking, friend, that's alright, though. My shipmates never understood why I seemed to care so much about her, either. I just liked to walk around and feel her different surfaces-- listen to the way her body adjusted itself to the ever- changing contours of the sea. It was wonderful. She liked me and she loved it when I laid my hands upon her. I couldn't have told you then just like I can't tell you now how I knew this but, nevertheless, I knew this.

On one of my strolls, around her, I met up with the captain. It was late in the evening, about an hour before midnight. I could just make out his silhouette at the wheel. Back in those days that's the way we steered the ships. We didn't have all of those fancy comput'n machines like you have, today.

I walked up to him and asked if it would be alright to join him. He just stood there, like some temple. I said, "It's beautiful out here, tonight, isn't it Capt'n?" He did not answer. The wind was rising, slightly, and it began to howl in our ears. We, the captain, the lady, and I, rose and fell with the waves. I remember the smell of the salt in the air, that night, it had been strong, too strong. Ain't it funny how you remember? It's funny how you remember.

I remember telling the captain how happy I was to have been selected for this trip but he did not respond. I remember asking him if anything was wrong and, again, he said nothing. I was getting ready to excuse myself and walk away when he finally said, "You love this ship don't you." It was clear that this was not a question but, rather, a statement of fact. Before I had a chance to reply, he continued to speak. He said, "I mean, you really love this ship. To you it's more than just a means of transport--to you it's almost alive." I nodded. "I see the way you walk around this vessel--see the way you listen when she speaks."

As long as I live, I'll never forget him say'n that, "when she speaks". It was as if he had been reading my mind. Nothing could be closer to the truth than what he had just said. I mean, sometimes, in the darkness, it sounded like she <u>was</u> speaking--talking to me and me alone, in a whisper. I remember the relief I felt when I realized that someone else, the captain no less, could hear her, too. I don't expect you to understand what I am speaking of, friend. Very few people know what I am talking about--very few, indeed, have heard the voice-- the calling; the alcoholic knows, though, the gambler and the smoker, alike, know, as well. Those who have a thirst that can't be quenched know, very well, what voice I am referring to, friend. Although this voice is neither man nor machine, it is familiar to all that hear. The captain said,

"This is not an ordinary craft, son, not ordinary in any way. It's a ship with a soul." I stood there, completely silent, while a cold chill ran through my being. I don't think I had ever given anyone more of my attention in my entire life. He went on. "Have you ever heard of an Ekkdah, boy?" I shook my head. "An Ekkdah," he continued, "is a ship with a soul. They are said to exist every hundred years or so. The ark was said to have been one."

"Is that why it survived the flood, Sir," I asked?

"Yes, I think so. No wooden ship, then or now, could have weathered such horrendous forces, naturally."

We stood there thinking for a while. The wind continued to gain strength and the captain had both of his hands on the wheel, now. I asked, "So then an Ekkdah is a good and protective spirit?"

"The one that saved Noah and his people was, I think. But, it is said that evil Ekkdahs exist, also."

"You mean some ships are possessed by the devil?"

"Well, I don't think "possessed" is the best way to put it. You see, the "evil" ones are those that try to perform some service--I don't know what, exactly, but, some service to the world. It is said that they care not about who or what they hurt or destroy in order to gain their objectives. Some tribes believe that these evil forces are spirits bound to the vessel until they rid the world of something it, the world I mean, does not need."

The wind died down and there was silence, total silence.

The captain said to me, "Do you hear it, son?"

"Yes, I do."

She was moaning. Perhaps moaning is not the best way to put it but you'd be hard pressed to find a better word. It was becoming harder and harder to see him in the darkness. He said, very quietly, "What do you think brought you here, on this voyage, I mean. You probably think you just got lucky or some such nonsense." Again, it was not a question. "You and I are not here by mere chance, my young friend, not by a long shot. I'll bet that if you put your mind to it you would find that all of us, every man on board, save one, has something very significant in common with each other. No, there is a reason for us being here--and I think, I think you'll be the one. There is always one left, you know."

"Sir," I said, "I'm afraid I'm not following you."

"Tell me a little about yourself, boy." I told him about myself--where I was from and the kinds I things I wanted to do when we returned home. He just listened, like some idle and then he turned and walked away.

I remember that after the captain and I finished speaking, I went to my bunk to have some sleep but sleep would not have me. I was awake that whole night thinking about her and what the captain had said. I thought about old Noah and his ark--I thought about the Ekkdahs and what they were said to be and do.

I remember feeling different about her after that conversation, very different. It was one thing for me to think of her as, well, as a living lady--known only to me as such but quite another to know that she was said to be some kind of ancient incarnation trying to atone for past transgressions against humanity. I don't know how but that conversation with the captain had, in some way, warped my feelings towards her.

The captain had said that everyone on board had something in common. I began to wonder what that commonality could possibly be. Although I had served with most of those men, on other ships, I didn't know any of them well enough to call my friend. Nevertheless, I did know who each man was, by name, and a little about his past. In those days ships were smaller--not like today's floating monstrosities and it would have been hard to have served with a man for very long without learning about him and his people. Sometimes, all there is to do on those long journeys is to talk to your mates about yourself and those whom you miss.

I can not remember their names for certain, now. It's been a long time. I do remember some of their stories, though. There had been a fellow—let's call him Jacobs on board. He had once been a military man. It was said that he had had a promising career in the service--a spotless record and all that. They said some one had made a bet with him and had lost. Jacobs forced the man to pay and, according to rumor, it had cost the man his life. It was said that Jacobs was a fugitive.

Another man on board—let's call him McCormick, it was said, had been a merchant seaman several years prior to our voyage. A ship he was serving on had gotten attacked by some African natives. He had been captured and beaten by the natives. After he had been released, by one means or another, he had met an African woman and they fell in love. She became pregnant. When the tribal elders learned of this fact, they kicked both of them out of their kingdom. McCormick and his wife had tried to make it to a neighboring village but, being with child, she did not make it. There had not been enough food for them and McCormick, not knowing the area, did not know how to get food for them. She died and McCormick had been found by some scouts. They say he had been two minutes from death, himself. Although he hardly ever spoke of these thing, you could see that he simply did not know how to live without her. Because she had been an African native, no white man took his loss seriously and thus no empathy was given him.

I remember that the man who had put his hand on my shoulder on the day we set sail was said to have been a blacksmith, at one time. They say he had had a dog, a dog that he loved very much. Some said he loved that dog more than his own life. It was rumored, if I remember correctly, that there had been a fire in a three-story building directly across from his blacksmith shop. I don't know how but it came down to him having to decide who he would save from the blaze, his dog or a little boy who was also trapped up there in the burning building. He chose to save the dog and the little boy was burned to a cinder. The town's people were outraged and thoroughly disgusted with his choice. A town meeting was held the results of which sent a group of men over to his home. The angry men, one of whom was the dead boy's father, took him and his dog into the woods and strung them both up side-by-side. At the last possible minute, before he gave up the ghost, they cut him down but they let his dog die. That had happened several years before I met him but I remember seeing the rope marks on his neck. I always got the willies every time I saw them. Somehow, I always felt as if I were speaking to a dead man whenever I talked to him. I see the look on your face, friend, and I agree, it is a

90

horrible thing to think but you have never seen a rope-marked neck, have you? I did not think so.

I seem to remember that one of my shipmates was said to have been widowed by an old girl friend who never got over him. They say she was into black magic and had vowed to curse the remainder of his days. Once, while we were eating together, he told me that he didn't believe in any of that stuff but he always kept some kind of good-luck charm hanging around his neck and, most likely, in his pocket, too.

And then there was the captain. They say he had been serving as captain on a ship, some years earlier, when a crewmember had died on board, mysteriously. They say that the crewman had threatened the captain's life the day before he died. No one knew, exactly, what had happened but they said that almost every other night, those who had quarters near the captain's cabin, could hear him cry out in the middle of the night--something about it not being worth the hell or some such thing.

Then there was me. I remember asking myself what I had in common with all of those men. It seemed to me that I had nothing in common with them. Everyone on board was running, in one way or another, from his past. They were trying to become lost. I, on the other hand, was not. My path was not littered with skeletons. The only thing about me that might be remotely interesting was that I was an orphan. An orphan! I remember how it hit me, like a ton of bricks, I can tell you. All the men on board were running from something--trying to become lost, in a sense. I, an orphan, had been lost, instead. If anything, I had always had the desire to know where I had come from--I and I alone was the only man on board trying to find his history--not loose it.

It must have been a week or so later when I next spoke to the captain. I was swabbing the deck when he approached me and said,

91

"I would like to speak to you, crewman." I walked with him back to his cabin and sat on a wooden chair. I remember wondering how many men must have sat on it scared to death of what the captain might say. I was not scared, however. I didn't know what he was going to say to me but I knew that it would have nothing to do with ship business.

He seated himself across from me, behind his desk, lit a cigarette, leaned back in his chair, put his feet up on to the desk and said, "How are you?"

"I'm fine, Sir," I answered cautiously.

"Do you feel alright?"

"Yes Sir. Is something wrong, Sir."

"No, no more than should be wrong. Have you been thinking about what we spoke of, last week I believe it was?"

"Yes Sir, I have."

"And what have you come up with?"

"Well, I'm not sure, I don't think I know yet." I remember thinking to myself that I should answer as ambiguously as possible. There had been reason for this approach but the years have a way of dimming the light of recollection. I guess that's why a man will make the same mistake twice, eh?

"Has she spoken to you recently?"

"No, Sir, not recently."

"Are you sure, son? It's very important that I know."

Neither of us said anything, for a while, and then I said, "Well, I don't know if I would call it speaking but something has changed--the sounds she makes are different, now. It seems, well, I don't know. Maybe it's just my imagination but it seems like the timbre of her voice has become more malevolent."

The captain became tense when I said this--I remember that very well. He said, "Yes, I've noticed that, too. I don't know much about these things but I think something is going to happen soon."

"What do you mean, Cap'n?"

"You have been thinking, haven't you, it's written all over your face--tell me, boy."

He was beginning to worry me, a bit. It was as if he could read my thoughts and I did not like that. Quietly I said, "Sir, I've been thinking and I believe I know what all of the men on this ship have in common."

Leaning back in his chair, he nodded, satisfied. He said, "I knew you had. Tell me, what binds us together?"

I related my observations and my opinions to him. I did not include him in my statements, however. When I had finished he asked, "And what of me? Have you not wondered why I
am the captain of this particular vessel?"

I said, "Well, some one had to be, Sir."

"Come now, I know you have fashioned some reason for my presence on this ship."

Again, I did not answer for a long while. Finally, I said, "Does it really matter, Sir?"

He looked at me for some time and said, "No, I suppose it doesn't."

"Cap'n?"

"Yes?"

"I know that I am different from the rest of you."

"Yes," he sighed, "I believe you are. You will be the one."

"The one for what?"

"That, too, doesn't matter. Remember, young crewman, keep us in your heart and we will continue."

"Sir?"

He leaned forward, grabbed a writing quill in one hand a piece of paper in the other and said, quite business like,

"You are dismissed, crewman."

Yep, it was just like that. He dismissed me without saying another word. What did I say? Why, I said nothing--I mean, back in those days when your captain told you that you were dismissed you didn't argue with the man.

I remember awakening the next day to the sounds of howling winds and storming seas in my ears. Based on the way the ship was being tossed about, I guessed that the waves must have been over a hundred feet high. As I made my way on to the bridge I heard some one yell, "Man overboard!" You know something, I had never heard those words uttered until then and I will never forget the terror they struck in my heart. Jesus! Would you go get me some water--I'm feeling a little shaky--no, no, I'm fine I just need to rest a bit.

There. That's better. Now, as I was saying, the sky was black with clouds and it had begun to rain. The ship was moving so violently that all of us were grabbing on to anything tied down to keep ourselves from joining our unfortunate crewmate in the cold sea. Thunder roared and lightening flashed above our heads. The sounds that the sea and the wind were making was, to say the least, enormous and horrible.

We were taking on water and I remember stepping into a pool of it and falling hard. Men were racing back and forth trying to keep the ship from loosing her integrity. It was terrible. Some one walked up to me with a bucket in his hand and yelled, "We've lost sight of him--the man who went over. Jesus! I can't believe this is happening!" His voice barely cut through the wind.

To make a long story short, we eventually got things under control and the storm subsided. Yes that's right, nothing mysterious happened, that time. When things on board began to get back to normal I returned to my quarters and thought very seriously about what the captain and I had discussed.

It must have been around four o'clock in the morning when I heard her. Now, I know that I am an old man and you will probably think that what I am about to tell you is the product of an old man's imagination but it is not! As surely as I am telling this story, what I am about to relate to you is the gospel truth.

As I said, it must have been somewhere around four in the morning when I heard it--her voice, I mean. I could hear her moaning--whispering to me. It was funny, for the first time I couldn't make out what she was trying to say to me. That scared me, it certainly did. I remember thinking that maybe the captain had been right. We had already lost one man and we had so far to go before the trip would be completed. I began to wonder if I would, in fact, be spared. I tried to listen more closely to what she was saying. The words became clearer and I found that I could, in fact, make out what she was saying. I don't know if I was actually hearing her words or if they were being placed in my mind but I guess it doesn't matter, in the big picture. As I listened I heard her saying, "Sing song, nothing's wrong, very soon, you'll all be gone." She kept repeating this over and over.

How did that make me feel? Let me tell you, it scared the hell out of me. It wasn't what she was saying that scared me the most it was the way she was saying it--as if she were not conscious of her words. I know that sounds crazy but it's true. It was a chant--a chant to fuel her will.

After I had deciphered what she was saying, I immediately went to see the captain. I went to his cabin but he was not there. So, I went in search of him and I found him on one of the lower decks sitting in front of some boxes. I held the lantern high so I could see him clearer. He was sitting on the floor with his head in his hands. Before I could open my mouth he said,

"You hear it, too, don't you." It was not a question.

"Yes, Sir, I do."

"Do you know what it means?"

"Yes, Sir, I think I do--I could be wrong, Sir--"

"No, no," he interrupted, "you are not wrong, son--God, I wish you were."

"What's going to happen to us?"

"What you really mean to ask is _how_ is it going to happen."

I said, "I thought that storm, the other day, was it, Sir."

"I can understand that but I knew that it wasn't."

"Cap'n," I asked?

"Yes."

"How is it that you know so much about this thing?"

He stood very slowly and said in a weary tone, "Because, my young friend, once upon a time I was you."

My mouth dropped open and I exclaimed, "You mean--"

"Yes," he cut in, "I was the only survivor on a ship bound for Hell."

"But Cap'n didn't you tell me that these types of things happens only once every hundred years or so?"

"Yes I did."

"Then how is this possible?"

He regarded me for a very long time. Finally, "Crewman, I said that they are believed to exist every hundred years or so but you can not legislate the will of an apparition."

"What are we going to do? We just can't sit around and wait."

"When I was on my first doomed ship there were some of us, even then, who knew what was going to happen. So, we tried to prepare--be ready to fight off fate. We checked every part of that ship to make sure nothing could go wrong. We took safety precautions that would have made the queen, herself, stand up and take notice. Believe me when I tell you that nothing, nothing we did made any difference. Everything we did only served to prolong the inevitable. I care about these men too much to do that."

"You said I am to survive, maybe. Is there something I can do?"

He smiled a wide, almost youthful smile and said, "My boy, you are only the messenger, the watcher, the witness. Some say that those who survive never tell what actually happens. I haven't, yet and I don't know why, exactly."

I'll never forget that day--the day that my life ended as I knew it.

"What happened?"

That's what I'm try'n to tell you. Just sit tight and let an old man think for a minute. I remember waking up on that day with an incredible headache. In fact, if I remember correctly, all of the men on board had some kind of unusual pain in their bodies. I remember that there was an enormous amount of thick black fog all around us--that's right, black fog.

My memories get kind of shaky here. I guess my subconscious doesn't want to remember this part, I don't know. It seems like all I can see, in my mind's eye, is that black fog--snapshots, that's the way these memories return to me, just like snapshots from a cheap camera. I remember standing at the helm with the captain. I remember him pointing to the east and turning to look at me. I remember the tears in his eyes. I remember the way my heart sank in my chest as I saw the rest of the men staring into the east. I remember the silence that fell over us. I remember the pain in my head, by this time it was becoming blinding. I------remember------seeing-------it--------feeling------it------her-------voice--------tha-------that--------

"Mr. Sims?"

No answer.

"Mr. Sims, what happened next?"

No answer.

The man presses on the call button and yells, "Nurse, nurse! Mr. Sims is not responding to my questions--he's not responding at all!"

A nurse enters the room and checks the monitors. She is an older lady and the man gets the feeling that she is very bitter about life. She says in an "I-told-you-so" manner, "I told you so. He's too old to be talking about that--that incident all over again."

"But ma'am," the man replies, "I have to learn what happened to my father--he was on that ship, you know. This is the only man on earth who knows what happened out there."

The nurse regards him for a moment and then speaks, choosing her words very carefully. She says, "Look, when my Frank was lost the boys and I went through a great deal of pain. I told them just like I'm telling you. It's time to get on with your life. I know you miss and have a need to be with your father but it's time that you put these things in your heart--not in your life. It's time for you to be a father to your own children. Do you have children, yet?"

The man lowers his head and answers, "Yes ma'am."

"You can not motivate your children to look forward to the future if you, yourself, keep looking backwards to the past. Do you understand?"

"Yes ma'am--but this man was there. No one's been able to figure out what happened on that ship. No one's been able to find any trace of it whatsoever. Mr. Sims was found floating on a raft fourteen knots from where he was supposed to be."

"I know," she replies, "but that happened many years ago and Mr. Sims has been in one kind of hospital or another ever since. Every time he tries to tell the story he goes into some kind of trance."

The man says, in a very soft voice, "It's as if there is some kind of spell over him or something."

"Oh, don't talk nonsense." She leans over her patient and wipes his forehead with a damp cloth. She says, "Maybe you can try again tomorrow."

"No, I've been searching for answers all of my life and I think it's time to stop. My own kids need me and I told myself that if I couldn't find out anything here, today, I would stop trying."
"No matter, if not you tomorrow, then some other person orphaned by that damned boat--what was its name, Blue Sea?"

"Blue-Night," he corrects.

She continues as if he hasn't said anything. "I've been here for many years and I have seen more relatives of the men who were lost on that ship come through here trying to find answers than I care to remember. It never ends."

The man walks to the door and turns to look at Mr. Sims. He asks the nurse, "Will he be alright?"

"Oh yes, he'll come out of it in an hour or so--don't you worry. Good luck to you, lad."

The man reaches for the doorknob. He thinks to himself, "Thank you for sharing your nightmare with me." He opens the door and leaves the room.

The nurse straitens the sheets around Mr. Sims. She sees a tear roll, slowly, down the side of his face. She whispers, "You old fool. Did you really think you could witness the passing and then tell the story? Sometimes I'm almost glad that my Frank did not survive--at least he was spared the hell, which you will have to live with for the rest of your life. You old fool. When will you ever learn?" She leaves the room and closes the door behind her.

The old man stirs in his bed, slightly. Behind his closed eyelids his pupils are dilated. Deep in his slumber, he

hears the screams of his shipmate--hears the
thunderous tearing of wood--hears his captain
screaming, "For God's sake, help me Siiiimmmmmmmss!!"

LETTER:
Do Not Drink And Drive
My Life Away

My Friend:

It is 3:37am and I am oh so very tired; that is why I am going to enumerate this reply to your voicemail message, OK?

1.
I received your text messages, in addition to your voicemail, earlier today but I was in the middle of posting a new article to my BLOG. Take a look at it, you may find it useful.

2.
Let me say that my plans have not changed. In fact, despite the way I feel about your atrocious behavior, it never occurred to me to not accompany you to your appointment, as I promised. When I give my word, I keep it. You should know me better than that by now.

3.
I am no longer angry just disgusted and very disappointed in you and your judgment, or lack there of.

As a pedestrian who was hit by an automobile, landing over twenty-five feet from where the skid marks stopped, because some idiot thought he was good to drive after an evening of guzzling down beers, I cannot adequately express my revulsion at the thought of you, over thirty years passed your age of majority no less, deliberately getting behind the wheel of a car after a night of sophomoric and pointless drinking.

Frankly, the thought of it sickens me and makes me weep for all of those who have lost and will lose their precious lives because of others who will selfishly, senselessly, criminally, and, in the end, viciously engage in such reprehensible behavior.

4.
As you frequently observe, I have proven, time and time again, how much I love you. What you should also know is that my love is not unconditional.

5.
In case you did not realize, my love is the world's most precious gift; a treasure deserved only by those who, among other things, treasure the lives of those they do not know and will never meet.

6.
Drunk driving is the action of one who is not worthy of my love, my compassion, my respect, nor my time.

7.
Unlike you and, sadly, so many of the world's population, I choose to be my proverbial neighbor's keeper even though my neighbor, most of the time, couldn't care less about me.

This is who I am and this is what I do; that is, place my neighbor's safety above my own convenience.

8.
As you read my words, ask yourself who you are and what do you want to do with the rest of your life. Regardless the answer, you will never be worthy of anything or anyone so long as you continue to drink and drive, placing your convenience above the safety of your neighbors, one of whom happens to be me.

That's right. Did you think about that? How would you feel if you were to plow into me as I cross the street because you were to inebriated to obey a traffic light? Are you really willing to put me, your one true friend, so needlessly as risk? Is my life and the lives of countless others worth less to you than a six-pack of beer, a fifth of whisky, or a bottle of wine?

9.

On behalf of all those whose lives you carelessly put at risk, I cannot forgive you for it is not my place to do so.

10.

I can, however, tell you that I have always valued your friendship and because of this, I will do whatever I can to help you face what will surely be your greatest challenge, yet.

11.

I will not abandon you so long as you acknowledge and accept responsibility for your reckless behavior, not by speaking silly little, pretty little words that will be carried away on the next puff of wind but by actions that will stand the test of time.

12.

This ordeal has definitely taxed the limits of our friendship. Nevertheless, unless or until you demonstrate that you do not truly regret your decision to drink and drive my life away, by doing it again, my love is with you.

That's The Way Love Goes.

THE PATIENT

(Patient)   "--But I'm tellin' you Doc', that's just the way it happened!"

(Doctor)   "Come now--lets stay calm about this. I really don't think there's a need to take <u>my</u> head off."

                   (A door opens behind the patient and a second doctor enters the room.)

(Doc 1)   "AH! Here we are--I'm glad you could make it, Doctor. Our patient, here, was just telling me about his (he frowns) <u>experience."</u>

(Patient)   "Experience-my-ass!"

                   (Both doctors look at each other, as if to say, "Yeah! Here we go again!" The second doctor seats himself a little to the left of the patient. The first doctor moves his chair further to the right of the patient. Both men take a deep breath and look directly at their quarry. The patient's head is slightly lowered.)

(Doc 2)   "I've read the reports on what you <u>claim</u> to be an after-life experience. I understand that unlike others who have experienced this phenomena, your experience was--" (He frowns, trying to find the most appropriate word.)

(Doc 1)   "Different."

(Patient)   "Jesus! You don't understand--you just don't understand!"

(Doc 1)   "Now then, lets take it from the top, shall we?"

(Doc 2)   "Yes--yes, the top is good. Lets take it from the top."

                       (The patient moans inwardly and shivers--and after taking a very deep breath, begins to recount the ordeal once again.)

THE LETTER

1

As he walked back into the room and sat his rather over plump derriere on the hard wooden chair at a small wooden desk he realized that he had been performing this same task, the one in which he was about to engage, for the past twenty-two years of his life. He was very disgusted with himself, to say the least. All that time and he still hated doing it--hated it with a passion.

2

Step, step, step. He paces back and forth and back and forth again. It's not easy--this waiting game--not easy at all. In fact he hates it--he hates more and more as each day each month each year passes by.

The waiting goes on and on and on.

3

Rip, rip. He tears, rather brutally, the first of several envelopes that have arrived for the inmates, today. He is required to read each one and inspect its contents. He is required to make red marks all across the pages in order to make reading the letters much more difficult for the recipient.

During the past several years, however, he has begun letting the letters slip through unread and unmarked. He hated reading someone else's mail. Now, however, that would have to change. Last week he'd been caught letting letters slip through unread and he had gotten a very aggressive warning regarding the imminent consequences of his actions should they continue. In short, he was told that he would be fired if he allowed one more letter to reach an inmate unmarked. This had scared him and infuriated him at the same time. He only had eight more months until his retirement.

He begins to read:

"Dear Daddy, Mommy and I have just..."

4

He lay on his bed, face down, with tears rolling. She had forgotten to write him this week. He knew that sooner or later this would happen. Nevertheless, the tears came, as he knew they would, also.

5

Here was a letter for that guy in L. block--the guy who had tried to commit suicide four times since his incarceration. It was generally known throughout the facility that #273 had been convicted of a crime that he had not committed.

This was the only inmate who received a letter every week since he arrived here--every single week without fail. It simply amazed him. No one in his own family including his wife of over twenty-five years would have been so diligent in this task should he had been the one serving time.

Because of #273's precarious emotional state, no one would mark up his letters with red ink. Receiving marked up letters always sent #273 into a deep depression followed by a suicide attempt. After a while the guards had just simply stopped reading his mail, altogether.

However, in light of this warning he had just received, he had no choice but to read #273's mail this week, as well. He was just too close to retirement to take a chance on messing up.

He tore the envelope open and began to read.

6

Sadness and despair engulfed him. She had forgotten to write and thus, she had forgotten him. Without her he simply didn't have the will to carry on. Death was his only way out of this. These were the thoughts that ran through his head as he saw the other inmates receive their mail for the week.

She was the one person out there who knew that he was not guilty. She had been his link to that knowledge and that world and without her that world fell more than a million miles away. He just didn't care anymore—death was the answer..

7

"My Dearest,

"This has got to be the most difficult letter I have ever written. There's no way around it so--I have met someone new and we have decided to be together.

"I know that I promised to wait for you but I'm lonely and I did not think you would be convicted. I was wrong. I know that some day you will get out and when you do I'm sure that you'll find someone else to love as I have.

"Please, try to remember the good times.

"I Love you."

8

He tries to read the signature but it has been smudged or something--perhaps by tears.

He sets the letter down on his small wooden desk. He feels, for the first time, sincere and complete sorrow for #273. No innocent man should have to endure such bad luck, he thinks to himself.

He thinks about his life and how fortunate he had been to meet and fall in love with a good woman who, one day, became his wife. He thinks about how, when he first joined the force, he had done something that wasn't completely above board and how he had gotten away with it because of his father's connections.

He thinks about all of the injustices he has seen during his long lifetime—thinks about all of the bad guys who got away and all of the basically good ones who were forced, like #273, to take their place. He thinks about pain and hunger and loneliness and despair. He thinks about his brother who one day, while crossing the street, had been hit by a car driven by a man more interested in his young blonde passenger than his driving. His brother had been blinded by the accident.

He thinks about the burned pizza he tried to heat up once when he and his wife had a spat that lasted three days during the course of which she had gone to stay with her sister. He had been forced to cook for himself. He remembers sitting alone at the kitchen table trying to pretend that everything was just fine. He remembers sitting there at the table, shoving piece after piece of the bitter tasting black crust into his mouth while his heart silently cried out to her to come home.

After all these years, sitting here at his little wooden desk, he cannot remember what the actual argument had been about but he does remember feeling foolish, childish, and above all afraid —afraid of losing the woman he loved.

He, the Iceman to his friends, begins to melt a little.

9

He was so deep in thought that he almost didn't hear the soft sound of an envelope land on the floor inside his cell. It had been three days since he had realized that she had forgotten him--three long dark and unfeeling days.

He knelt down and picked the envelope up off the floor and opened it. As his eyes gazed upon the page he was relieved to see that it had not been marked up. He began to read:

"Dearest,

"I have missed you and..."

10

He places the letter under his cot. Life was worth living again. She has not forgotten him--in fact it appears that she needs him as much as he needs her. So, he decides that he will be strong, in this place, as much for her sake as his own. She still believes in his innocence and that knowledge fills him with joy and hope for the future.

11

Sitting in his car, at a red traffic light, on his way home, he wondered why he had done what he had done. Why had he placed that final letter from #273's lady-friend in his permanent file and written a new one? Why had he taken up where she had left off?

As he turned into the driveway of his home the answer came to him. The answer was simple. Sometimes we have to love others as much as we love ourselves. Sometimes we must stop seeing the hate and start feeling the hurting of others.

In a year's time #273 would be up for parole and he vowed to be there--to make sure the real story got told, this time around.

Upon his release, #273 will be given that final letter and hopefully by then he will be able to deal with it a little bit better.

Being kind for mankind's sake is the noblest of deeds. Allowing himself to feel altruistic love for #273 made him feel good. Helping to make #273's burden a little easier to bear made his own burdens easier to bear, as well because "That's The Way Love Goes."

LETTER:
That's What Friends Are For

Dearest,

You are more than welcome for this little token of my affection.

You know, so often during the course of a day, week, month, year, etc, one can forget her value in life. As one deals with the day-to-day trials and tribulations of both work and family, it is so easy to forget that she is someone special and, as such, touches the lives of so many in very extraordinary and wonderful ways.

Sweetie, to this very day, you are among the very, very few in my life who has always made me feel unique and appreciated; it is a very rare gift that I will always hold close to my heart.

So then, perhaps you will understand when I say to you that I have more to thank you for than you, me.

Honey, never forget that, on your worst day, you are more warm, kind, caring, genuine, and gracious than most people are, on their best.
You must never allow anyone or anything to rob you of this knowledge.

Sugar, believe in yourself and there will always be those who believe in you, just as I.

Even though I do not say it often enough, I value your friendship a great deal.

My grandmother used to say to me, "Treat good people in your life like gold, treasure them always."

My friend, you are a very good, good person.

If there is ever anything I can do to help you in anyway, please do not hesitate to let me know; after all, that's what friends are for.

COMIN' HOME

And she also notices that there is a chill in the air, too. "I'm cold," she thinks to herself, as she walks.

The big Greyhound pulls away, its diesels wheezing their way in to the night.

There are tears in her eyes. She has over a mile and a half to walk before she will reach the bus station. She had insisted that the bus driver allow her to get off the bus, here, a mile and a half outside of the little town where she had grown up, because she needed time to think--needed a little more time to sort things out.

As she walks, she remembers the expression on the bus driver's face when she said to him, "I need to get off, now, please." His expression had been one of deep and abiding empathy, which, now that she thinks about it, seemed a little too polished to be believed. She supposed he had thought that she had needed to throw-up or something. He had stopped the bus without asking her a single question. She stepped off. The bus waited. Realizing that the bus would continue to wait until she reboarded, she looked up into the bus and into the driver's eyes and said, "Thank you, I'll be fine." She waved him on. His mouth dropped open, in surprise, at her request--he was about to protest when she turned and began walking, slowly, away.

The diesels dozed while the driver decided what to do next. She kept walking. She could feel his gaze and those of his passengers burning into her back. She kept walking. Finally--mercifully, the tired diesels stood to attention, once again, and the big bus began to roll.

And now, she is walking, alone, down a dirt road, which leads to a small bus station in a small town, which used to be her home. The town, towards which she is now walking, the place where she had grown up, has not seen her form for over thirteen years--thirteen long years.

Her head lowered, she whispers, "Thirteen years," over and over and over again. It's been thirteen years since she ran out of her mother's house vowing never to return. It has been thirteen years since her mother had found her, in the kitchen, caressing the hand of a fellow schoolmate, who, to her mother's astonishment, was also female.

She stops walking for a moment, looks up into the dark cloud-covered sky and sighs, softly. She can feel the town getting closer--feel the weight of the backwardness settle over her as it approaches.

She looks at the two small bags, one in each hand, and thinks, "After all this time, this is all I have to bring back-- just a few stupid gifts?"

She begins to walk, again.

She had tried to explain to her mother but her mother had been too busy, first yelling at the girl and then throwing her out of their house. She had tried to tell her mother that they had just been bored and curious and nothing more.

The memory runs clear and hard in her mind as she walks.

"What in the hell is wrong with you, girl?" Rage, disgust and horror saturates her mother's every word.

"What the hell were you doing that for? This is a God fearing house and we do not--repeat, do not touch members of our own gender in that way!"

No answer.

Getting no response, her mother continues, "What would people think if they found out?" It was more of a statement than a question.

The lecture her mother embarked upon seemed endless. It went on and on and on. At one point, during this oration, her mother's hand had come from out of nowhere and hit her in the face. Her mother struck her three times, the last of which sent her reeling into the kitchen wall.

The tears begin to roll down her cheeks, as she walks.

The shame and sadness she had felt on that day, so long, long ago, had almost destroyed her. Even now, she found it difficult to believe that she had done such a thing.

The girl whom her mother had caught her touching had been just a casual friend. Everyone in town suspected that she and her family were "different" but no one knew for sure--people just generally stayed away from them.

Now she can see the outline of the little town, in the distance--closer and closer.

She had only rubbed the girl's hand, well--maybe stroked was more accurate but that had been the extent of the experience. She had not, particularly, enjoyed it, either--a fact that she tried and tried again to convey to her mother and the rest of her family and her few remaining friends and finally, the township, itself. No one believed her.

Even after all these years, she still did not know, for sure, how the word had gotten out about her and that girl. She suspected that her mother, having never kept a secret in her entire life, probably let it slip. The news about her spread like wildfire throughout the town. That exact same fire burned away any hope of her leading a normal life in that town.

The smells of the town reach out for her as she nears--
smoke, hay, bacon, flowers, manure, gasoline, and
much, much more.

The girl whom she had been "found with", as her mother
came to regard it, had moved away a short time
afterwards--her father had gotten a job in a different
state, or so they said.

She walks faster, now, faster. She hears faint sounds
from the town--a dog barking, someone slamming a lid
down on a metal trashcan or something, a car engine
backfiring, and a cricket singing.

"Why am I doing this?" she asks herself as she crosses
the town-line. Her life, as an adult, is a relatively normal
one. She fights traffic, she goes to work, she comes
home and prepares dinner, she eats dinner, she goes to
bed and does it all again the next day. She pays her
taxes.

She is currently seeing, casually, a nice young man
whom she met at a singles-only party. Why then must
she return to this place--the place that tried to label her
as something she was not? Why had she decided to
take a bus instead of her nice new car? She supposed
the answer to that last question was simple enough.
She had left this town on a bus and so, for some strange
reason, it seemed only right to return here in the same
way.

Only a few more blocks, now--a few more blocks until
she reaches the bus station. The bags are heavy in her
hands and her heart is heavy in her chest. She is, to her
own disbelief, scared.

She turns right on to Main Street. There, a red, white,
and blue neon sign proclaims that it sits upon the roof of
the Greyhound bus station.

Memories of rejection and cruelty done to her dance in
her mind. Each step she takes, now, is accompanied by

a remembered event of relentless persecution--the girls making fun of her in school, the boys pointing fingers at her at dances and laughing, the whispers of the congregation as she entered the church for Sunday service, the rocks thrown at her, the dirty filthy notes stuck to her locker-door, the obscene gestures, the shame she saw in her mother's eyes whenever she walked into a room where her mother was entertaining guests. There had been more, so much more.

The memories slam into her as she walks down the sidewalk. She can feel their impact upon her spirit and they weaken her almost to the point of collapse. Somehow, however, just as she did thirteen years ago, she finds the strength and the courage to keep walking.

She was glad she'd gone--glad she had decided to leave this crap-filled backwards thinking, culturally stunted town.

It had been hard at first--hard to find food or a place to stay where she would not be assaulted. She had done it; however, and in addition she had managed to get her G.E.D. She had then gotten a job as a nanny from one of her teachers. Since then, she had managed to earn enough money to go to college and earn her degree. Now, she is the author of two best-selling children's books and her future is bright.

One block to go.

No matter how successful she becomes, however, there had always been this unfinished business here, in this town--some unsettled issues that must be put to rest. She was not coming home for her mother's sake or for the sake of her friends. She was coming home, to the past, for her own sake.

As she walks up to the glass door of the bus station it is opened, from within, by a rather large, weatherworn-featured woman who looks at her and says, "So, you're finally comin' home."

She loves her life and she has come to understand and love herself, as well. It is because of this self-appreciation that has compelled her to face and conquer the only monster in her past. She knows that she will only be able to fully embrace the future when she has fully accepted the past. It is love that will make this possible. It is love that makes this necessary because "That's The Way Love Goes."

A BREAKFAST MOMENT

"No Mama!" the teary-eyed seven-year-old boy cries as his mother's closed fist jets through the air towards him. "No!" Her rock-hard fist makes contact with his tiny fragile face and he crashes backward into the wall.

"I'm so sick of you," She yells at the half dazed seven-year-old little child lying on the floor. "I'm so tired of having to watch you all the time because you can't see. Why did you have to be born blind? What did I do to deserve this?"

She walks over to him. Sensing her approach, he instinctively raises his little hands to defend against another unseen crushing blow. With desperation in his frightened little voice, her child pleads, "But I can see, Mama, just not as good as everybody else, I really can."

His words make her stop, unclench her fists, and think about what she is doing. She looks down at her baby boy and sees fear, the fear she's forced upon him, reflected in his innocent blameless face. She kneels down, gently pulls him up towards her, and holds him. They cry together. She says, sobbing, "I know you can see a little but it's not enough. You keep bumping into things, hurting yourself, and breaking stuff. I get so tired. Sometimes I wish you had never been born. At least then you wouldn't suffer so and I wouldn't have to see you suffer."

The young boy says, pulling back from her but still crying, "But Mama, I'm not suffering. My eyes don't hurt unless you hit me. I'm sorry I knocked over the coffee table again. I won't do it anymore."

1

"Ok," his mother says, seating herself at the breakfast table, "everybody dig in."

He, his mother, his ten year old brother, his mother's two sisters, and his four cousins are sitting at a dark brown mahogany table in the middle of a rather small cozy kitchen with a low ceiling. He and his five junior contemporaries are wearing their various cartoon superhero pajamas and the three women are wearing plain simple Midwestern dresses.

His mother's older sister, whom he thinks of as big aunt because of her huge soft mushy tummy, asks, "Who wants some eggs?"

"I do," he says eagerly lifting his empty plate towards the sound of her voice.

"Put that plate down boy," his mother commands impatiently, "the last thing I need is to have to clean up something you knock over." His cousins giggle.

He immediately lowers his plate back to the table with both his appetite and his enthusiasm for the meal and his relatives, respectively, slowly draining away.

His mother's younger sister, whom he thinks of as snooty aunt because of her incessant bragging about her husband, her two little girls, her in-laws, her neighborhood, her house, her furniture, her yard, her gardener, her car, her jewelry, her clothes, her weight, her body, her hair, her skin complexion, her cooking, her cookware, her friends, her doctors, her regularity, and anything else she can lay claim to says to him, "You just wait. We'll get to you. Just sit there and be still."

The rectangular country style kitchen is bathed in morning sunlight let in by two big windows on either side of the table. At one end stands an old brown vintage refrigerator accompanied by a large single sink. At the other end of the room stands a much-used dark green gas stove with four burners beside a tall glass paneled china cabinet. The room is filled with the comforting aroma of freshly brewed coffee.

Big aunt begins ladling out heaping mounds of hot scrambled eggs to his cousins who, to both his and his brother's disappointment, are all girls.

One of his cousins says, "Can someone pass the bacon?"

The plate of bacon begins its slow journey around the table. As it moves from person to person, its delicious cargo is reduced by two and three pieces at a time. As it approaches him, he raises his uncertain little hand to take a piece but his mother, seeing this, raises the plate over him and passes it to his brother, instead.

His mother says to both of his aunts, "He's always trying to do things he can't see well enough to do and he's always knocking things over."

His youngest cousin, who is four years old, says to her mother, "That's because he's blinder than a bat, right Mommy?"

Everyone, including the adults, laughs. Well, not everyone; the embarrassed hurt little seven-year- old boy doesn't laugh; no, he doesn't laugh at all.

2

Hello God. I am sorry for not talking to you lately but I've been so sad. As I guess you already know, I made Mama mad today when I knocked over a plant in the living room. I didn't mean to do it. She keeps it so dark in there and she's always moving things around. I try to remember where everything is but sometimes I forget when I'm running. I can see, though, I really can. I just can't see as well as my brother and everybody else.

Please forgive me for making Mama mad today. Forgive her for hitting me. She doesn't mean to be so mean; she's just mad at me for being blind. But, I'm not really blind I can see, just not as good as, well, you know.

I've been sad God because lately some of the kids in the neighborhood have been picking on me. You know, they throw rocks at me and hit me in the head and then they run just far enough away so I can't see them. It's not fair, God; it's so not fair. Why can't I see like everybody else, Lord? They say in church that you love everyone but if that's true then why do you not let me see good? Don't you love me like you love everyone else?

My brother runs away with them and when I ask him to tell me who threw the rocks, he won't tell me.

I know it's wrong to hate people but, sometimes, I really hate my mother and my brother. She likes him better than me. She tells me that all the time. If I could see better, I would run away from this place.

She says it's my fault that my father left her. She says that he blames her for giving birth to a blind mutant. What's a blind mutant, Lord? Oh well, I guess it doesn't matter. Whatever it is, I guess I'm it. She says that I ruined her life and the life of my brother. Please forgive me for doing that, Lord, please. I didn't mean to be born blind.

I wish my grandmother was still here. Why did you take her away? Is she happy now? If you don't understand everything I've said, just ask her to explain it to you. She really understands me. She knows I can see but just not as well as everybody else. Tell her I said "hey."

Tomorrow, my aunts and my cousins are coming to visit for a couple of days. I don't like it when they're here. Everybody always treats me like I'm stupid just because I can't see well. I'll be glad when they leave.

I love you Lord. Goodnight. Amen.

3

"There," his mother says, setting his plate of bacon and eggs down in front of him. "Now try not to make a mess." He picks up his fork and knife and slowly begins to eat his breakfast.

"Anyway," snooty aunt says to his mother while putting a fork full of country fare in her mouth, "that's what happens when you marry a good hardworking educated man like I did."

His mother lowers her head in shame.

"It's not her fault," big aunt chimes in, "she always did make dumb choices and pick losers even when we were kids, remember?"

The children are all eating now and, other than the voice of the current speaker, there are only the sounds of utensils scraping against thick heavy long-used cream-colored plates.

"Yeah," snooty aunt replies. She adds, "Remember that time when she tried to cheat on that reading test in school? She copied the answers from the dumbest girl in class."

His four cousins and his brother laugh.

His four-year-old cousin asks innocently, "Mommy, when are we going to the zoo so I can see what a black sheep looks like?"

Her mother, big aunt, looks at her sharply and snaps, "Be quiet."

"But Mommy," the little one says, confused, "you said she's the black sheep of the family, didn't you?"

Six junior size hands reach out and pick up six jelly jars full of orange juice and tip them back towards six open and waiting junior size mouths.

After returning his glass to the table his brother, sitting on his left says, "Hey, where's the toast?"

The rest of the children echo his question by saying, in unison, "Hey yeah."

His mother, seizing the opportunity to take herself off the path of her sisters' little stroll down memory lane, quickly stands and walks over to where the bread is setting and begins depositing slices in to the toaster. Looking back at her older son she says, "Get up and get the jelly out of the refrigerator." His brother complies.

4

Returning to the breakfast table, his mother sets a plate of hot toast beside two jars of jelly. Sitting back down next to him she says, "Who wants some strawberry jelly on their toast?" It's my favorite."

Big aunt answers, "I'll take the grape. I can't stand that strawberry stuff you buy." His four cousins declare, in a rather humorous staccato, "Me too."

Snooty aunt says to his mother, "You never did have good taste in anything. Do you really like that strawberry stuff? Here, let me do it." She takes the knife his mother was about to use and opens the jar containing the grape jelly and begins spreading it onto a slice of toast.

He can feel his mother's embarrassment and uneasiness returning yet again. He can tell that she wants to say something in her own defense but, as always, when dealing with her two siblings, she does not.

Snooty aunt looks at his brother and says, "Ok, it's your turn, my one and only handsome young nephew. Which one do you want, the strawberry or the grape?"

His brother responds without any hesitation whatsoever, "The grape please. I don't like the strawberry either."

Finally, after taking care of everyone else first, she looks at him and says with an air of triumph over his beleaguered mother, "Ok, let's see which one our little blind man will choose. Which one would you like? Now there are two jars of jelly on the table in front of you. One jar is strawberry jelly and the other is grape jelly. So, which one will it be?"

Now he, like everyone else at the table, absolutely hates strawberry jelly. He, like everyone else at the table, only wants grape jelly. Unlike anyone else at the table, however, he, this belittled and berated and emotionally ignored and completely unwanted precious seven-year-old visually impaired child can feel his mother's pain; and in that moment, that one incredible breakfast moment, feels sorry for her and love for her.

After a short pause he says with absolute confidence, "I want the strawberry jelly. I can't stand that grape stuff. It's disgusting. Once, it even made me sick at my tummy. My mom knows what's best and she and I always eat the best and the best is strawberry not grape."

Snooty aunt's mouth falls open.

His mother, for the first time since his birth, reaches over and takes his hand and doesn't let go.

5

No one ever knew what happened in that moment, that breakfast moment, as he came to think of it many years later; no one except, of course, he and his mother.

Even now, when he sits in his big soft leather executive chair located at the headquarters of the company he built, he finds himself thinking about it from time-to-time. No matter how many years go by, he remembers that breakfast moment and asks himself why, after all the mean and cruel things she'd done to him when he'd needed her the most, he had sided with her.

"Because that's the way love goes," he says in a soft whisper.

"Sir?" his west coast division executive secretary asks as she guides him through a dimly lighted five star hotel lobby, on the way to a meeting with his board of directors. "What did you say?"

"Oh nothing," he says with a sigh, "I was just thinking about something that happened many years ago, from my youth."

ONE MAN LAND

And I am walking in it.

It is foreign yet familiar.

It is puzzling yet pleasant.

And I am walking in it.

It is dark and damp.

It is dry and crisp.

And with each step I take, I move everywhere and nowhere.

I try to utter a sound but am stifled by my own wonder.

And I am walking in it.

I can not see for the light is too bright, too dark.

Fear rules this place; not happiness or love, fear.

Fear of falling and the fear of hurting, too.

The fear of being alone and lonely.

Here, terror is king.

These are the walls with which I have surrounded myself.

And within these walls I must live.

These walls are thick.

Yet, although these walls are thick, under a friend's hand they would fall.

But friends are hard to find; even rare.

Rarer still are those that will lend a hand.

And that is why I live in this one man land.

JAX LANDING

Cameo of two men sitting in an office:

The office is located in the psychiatric ward of an as yet unknown institution. The first man, seated in a large dark brown leather chair behind an auspicious and intimidating mahogany desk, is dressed in a slightly rumpled light grey suit, with a white shirt and maroon-colored tie. The top of his desk is hidden beneath several rolling hills and valleys of papers, files, books, pens, pencils, general office supplies, and a rather impressive assortment of various communication and recording devices. One of these devices has a slowly blinking red light indicating that it is performing its task.

The second man, dressed in a simple plain navy blue uniform resembling hospital scrubs, is seated on a very uncomfortable armless straight-backed wooden chair that creaks with each movement of his body.

The man behind the desk is speaking to the man on the chair with an obvious air of condescension and contempt. As he listens, the man in the navy blue uniform, with clinched teeth and closed eyes, turns his face up towards the ceiling in frustration. After a few moments, he lowers his head in defeat. The man behind the desk is silent now, obviously waiting for a reply. Finally, the man in the simple plain navy blue uniform looks up at his opponent and slowly nods.

The man in the light grey suit opens a drawer in his desk and removes a small shiny black object about the same shape and size as a deck of playing cards. He closes the drawer, stands and walks slowly around to the front of his desk and offers the device to the man sitting on the wooden chair. The man in the simple plain navy blue uniform reluctantly accepts it.

The discussion is over.

Is this thing on? I hope so. I never used one of these things before. It looks simple enough. That idiot shrink back there in the office told me to use this thing. He said it might help me remember what I've done. I don't know who is ever supposed to hear this but I guess it doesn't matter.

Whoever you are, I am recording this on a gadget that doesn't use tape. The doctor calls it a digital recorder. I guess us fifty-one year old guys are a bit out of touch with the latest technology, eh? A digital recorder, nope, I've never heard of anything like it before. I'll tell you what, you can keep your compact discs and your cell phones because I'll take a good old eight-track tape player any day and time, buddy. This digital recorder, yeah it's very small and as I said, it looks simple enough to use. In fact, it's so small that I can completely close my hand around it; come to think of it, if someone were looking at me, they would think I'm talking into my fist; anyway, enough about that.

Well, to tell you the truth, I don't really know where to begin. Do I describe where I am and what my room looks like? I really don't know what I'm supposed to say. Ok, I am sitting on my bed which is located in a small room in what I think is a kind of prison hospital; at least, I think it's a prison but I'm not sure. To be honest, they won't tell me what kind of place this is.

What I do know is that I am not allowed to leave this place and, with the exception of this room, I am under constant surveillance. Getting back to the description of this room; well, as I said, there is one bed in here just big enough for one person. In fact, I'd call it a cot rather than a bed. The walls have dark brown paneling and there are no windows. The floor is a dull white. Did I mention that there is no carpet? I think I did but I can't remember. I don't know how to make this thing play back what I've said yet. I'll figure it out later, I guess. Anyway, on one side of the bed is a white metal chair. I have not tried it yet. On the other side of the bed there is a white metal table with one drawer. Oh, on the table is a very regular looking lamp that doesn't throw out much light but I guess it'll have to be enough. At one end of my room is the door leading out into the hallway and at the other end of my room is the bathroom. Oh yeah, now that I'm looking at it, there is a small window in the door leading to the hallway. Just to the left of the door leading out to the hallway is a button I can press if I want to call someone. I guess it's a kind of intercom system. Who the hell knows?

I wonder how long the batteries in this damn thing last. Now that I think about it, I wonder if it even runs on batteries. Who knows, this thing may run on bad breath. If that's the case, then this new fangled digital recorder will have enough energy to last a lifetime. I guess you can't tell but I'm grinning. I got to find something to smile about, right?

Let's see, what else? Oh yeah, the bed stinks. It has one pillow but it's so flat that it might as well not be there at all.

What more would you like to know? Would you like to know what I look like? Well, use your imagination. Maybe I'll describe myself later on.

Oh, my name is Jax, Cecil Jax to be exact. Just call me Jax; everyone does.

This may be hard for you to believe but I swear it's the truth, I don't know why I am in here. Three days ago, I woke up on this very bed I'm sitting on right now. I woke up dressed in these clothes that they must have put on me while I was unconscious.

About twenty minutes after I first woke up in this room, a fellow dressed in a white uniform came and took me to see that doctor I just finished a "session" with. The doctor's name is Lesley, Raymond Lesley. Now tell me that isn't a kind of sissy name. Yeah you guessed it, I'm grinning again.

Anyway, during that first session, I kept asking him why I'm here and where, exactly, here is. I'm not sure how he did it but he always managed to get out of answering the question. God I hate shrinks. They never talk straight. They keep trying to get you to "discover the answers within yourself." What a load of crap.

Anyway, it's been three days and all I have been able to get out of him is that I am in this place, in some way, for my own protection and the protection of others. He told me that I am suffering from a kind of selective amnesia and that little by little they will all come to me, the answers I mean. He told me that when I finally realize what I've done, that day will be the scariest day of my life. God I hate that guy.

He is right about one thing, though, I am having trouble remembering things about my past and about my life. I do recall a conversation I had with my late uncle one time, when I was about thirteen years old, in which he gave me some advice that I have always remembered. He said to me, "There will be times in your life, boy, when you will lose your footing and the world will not make sense. It will appear that everyone and everything is against you and that you have nowhere to run. That's ok because you should never run, boy, never run. When that time comes and you feel you've lost your way, remember what I'm telling you here today. When you lose your footing and you fall, jump up and land squarely on both feet. When you land, stand tall and focus, focus. Remember that you are a man, a good man who can't be stopped. When you land, face the world and make it face you. You see, boy, it's not the fall that matters, it's the landing."

Yeah, after all these years, I still remember that and I guess I always will.

You know, I don't know what's going to happen tomorrow or for that matter, what's going to happen later today but I do know three important irrefutable facts; I know my name, I know that I was born in Candle Shore, California, and I know that no matter what it takes I'm going to figure out what the hell is happening to me and why I am in this place.

Even though I know he will never hear these words I want to say the following to my uncle, "Uncle Alfred, don't worry, I just made a perfect landing."

PERFECT LOVE (1)

My Love,

Never in my wildest dreams did I think I would find you.

But some how, some way, I did for you are here, in my life.

In those moments when you and I lie together, stars crossed in the midnight sky, bodies crossed in the midnight hour, I know that I have, at long last, found perfect love.

While I know that neither you nor I are perfect, what joins us, the chemistry, the magic, the respect, the admiration, the awe, the life-force itself, transcends perfection and cradles our combined glory in ethereal splendor.

Thoughts of being parted from you make me miss you even when such thoughts are inspired by mere imagination.

I know you feel the same because when you touch me, your touch is softer than soft, sweeter than sweet, deeper than deep, hotter than hot, and more blessed than blessed could ever be,

Words are not clear enough, dreams are not long enough, desires are not powerful enough, consciousness is not wise enough to explain what we have.

For what we have is that which has never been before nor shall ever be again, perfect love; and, my eternal companion, "That's The Way Love Goes."